This Book is

you are intrigued by reincarnation, love historical dramas, or want to know more about how the spiritual world works.

Karma and reincarnation are explained through the story from the 18th century Versailles Court of Louis XV to modern day Brighton.

❁

To
dear Gertrude

Enjoy!

Mary Bishop
x x

What people are saying

An excellent style, one that keeps you wanting to read more. I am so glad that you have written it. It will be a lesson for many. GC.

Ostensibly this is a work of fiction. But is it? It rings very true. The author is telling the story of past life adventures and their consequences in the present. Most readers however will see it as fiction. It reads well either way. There is a story that is interesting in its own right - can be read just as a story - but contains deep spiritual truths. It's the most enjoyable way to learn.

There are 3 parts to the book. Part 1 introduces us to the cast of characters in King Louis XV's palace in Versailles. The characters are all prominent people. They are of good families and are either personally involved in the King's court or members of the family of people involved. There is so much corruption going on - so many intrigues - so much underhandedness - that one wonders how anything ever got done. Terrible things happen here - betrayal, tragedy, assaults and even murder.

Part 2 deals with the after life - as the characters pass over. It is a beautiful portrait. All is love. Bitter enemies in life are reconciled. Each of the characters undergoes a life review - but this is a non judgemental affair - conducted by the Elders. In this higher state of consciousness each of the characters sees the failings of the previous incarnation and sees what needs to be done.

In Part 3 the same characters reincarnate in modern England. The spiritual connections of the past are still active. They are drawn to each other by ties that are stronger than steel. Some reincarnate in the same family. Some are married to each other. Unrequited love in Versailles becomes consummated now. A wound in a past life appears as a sensitivity in the present one. Every one gets together to work out their past karmas. Everything gets adjusted. I really enjoyed reading this book. I had trouble putting it down. There are deep truths expressed here but very easy to read. She shows rather than tells. She only deals with two lifetimes in this work. But imagine this multiplied many fold. Most people have had hundreds and even thousands of of incarnations. Each life is a continuum of many, many other and on going. A well written and enjoyable read. JP

I love the story and enjoyed reading the book very much. Most people have heard of reincarnation in these enlightened times. I think a wide and varied audience would appreciate this story, it has history, spirituality, and eternal questions – what's not to love? The characters are believable and interesting, as are the time periods, especially Versailles. I feel people would enjoy it immensely, as I said above, who doesn't want to dream they've lived before? It's an alluring theme. JL.

About the Author

Mary has worked professionally over the last 35 years in the field of holistic and spiritual work: writing, teaching, giving readings, workshops and working at festivals to empower others. To find out more about Mary, please visit **www.marybishop.co.uk** or contact **mary@marybishop.co.uk**

Mary's first book 'Alchemy of the Soul – learning to dance with your own Divinity' and her second book 'What Am I Doing Here? A Journey through Gaia' are available through Mary's website.

Living with her husband, Nigel, in West Sussex, Mary enjoys watching sunsets, catching up with friends and enjoying a glass of Chablis.

Associate of the London College of Psychic Studies.

Dedication

To my husband, Nigel,
and to my son, Aden.

Acknowledgements

To my husband Nigel who proof reads my books and has supported my writing career throughout. To Helen Colbeck who has also proof read my book and offered her on going encouragement.

To Nina Ashby for writing the Foreword for me.

To the Susan Mears Literary Agency and Hayley O'Keeffe for her work in helping me achieve publication.

To Chris Day of Filament Publishing who has guided me through the intricacies of the publishing world and published this book.

To George Curzon & Joe Polansky who read and wrote reviews for me.

One Life is not Enough

A powerful story of karma
and reincarnation
from Versailles to Brighton.

Mary Bishop

Published by
Filament Publishing Ltd
16, Croydon Road, Beddington,
Croydon, Surrey, CR0 4PA

www.filamentpublishing.com
+44(0) 20 8688 2598

One Life is not Enough
by Mary Bishop

Contents

'It is no more surprising to be born twice than once; everything in nature is resurrection'.
Voltaire

'For every action, there is an equal and opposite reaction.'
Issac Newton's 3rd law of physics.

'The lamps are different but the light is the same'.
Rumi

Foreword

Written with panache in the tradition of Dion Fortune, Mary Bishop regales us with a compelling story based on two lives time-lines of intertwined relationships, illustrating Spiritual Truths of the consequences for one's actions through time and space. The author, authoritatively versed in matters Spiritual, presents the principles of reincarnation, life after death and the persistence of patterns called 'karma', in an easy-to-understand way, through storytelling.

It feels like a channelled piece of writing. The characters are detailed, relatable, and convincing, and the clusters of relationships believable from first encounter to the end of the tale in another time and place. The historical settings are authentic and well described and the language used time appropriate. I highly recommend this book as a 'good read' with added value!

**Nina Ashby, BA, MBSP, Dip.Hyp, Author,
Former President of the British Astrological
& Psychic Society**

Introduction

This story is one of karma and how it affects others and of reincarnation where the consequences are felt and understood.

Karma: so what is it?

Karma, as with Newton's law of action and reaction, is the spiritual principle of cause and effect where intent and actions, and the results of those actions of an individual, influence the future of that individual and others around them. In other words, a spiritual law of what we give out will be returned to us one way or another.

We can equate karma to the old adage, "You reap what you sow" for good or bad.

Every event in our lives has a cause and effect and the consequence of the effect is an outcome that can be understood. If there are difficult consequences, we can learn from this experience and if we do, then that situation has been resolved and we will not have to live through it again.

Likewise, any kindness, a helping hand, a loving thought or even a smile can assist another soul on their difficult journey here.

So in essence, karma is an accountability - we are all responsible for our own behaviour and thoughts, both spiritually and materially. Awareness of our own spiritual level and life and the choices we make, all matter.

Reincarnation:

Once our lifetime on Earth is finished, I believe we go back to the spiritual realm and assess what we have achieved; explore what is unresolved and what matters need further work from us, which we do by reincarnating in a new life on Earth.

Sometimes at the end of a lifetime, the consequences of some events are left unresolved. This is called negative karma, and it therefore may be necessary to reincarnate with the same people again in order to rectify matters.

With negative karma we may retain anger, sorrow or other unhelpful vibrations which need to be resolved before we can move on and grow further as spiritual beings.

Pre-birth contracts can also be drawn up with other people during our visit back to the spiritual realm. A pre-birth contract with another person is a way of dealing with negative karma. It is an undertaking to go through a challenging experience and resolve any issues with the other person or people involved. It could be that the other person causing issues, may well be a friendly soul helping you to learn.

Reincarnating with a pre-birth contract gives us the opportunity to resolve difficulties by putting love into the situation rather than anger or bitterness. If we try to respond to the situation with love and compassion, then we are balancing karma by understanding and resolving the opposite side of the situation.

The spiritual realm though cannot interfere with our choices as we have free will too, so we can choose not to go through certain experiences again. This may mean we take the longer, scenic route of learning if we choose not to rectify the unresolved matters of the past when we arrive back on the Earth plane again.

Part 1

Chapter 1

Versailles 1739 - 1746

The child was born in the August of 1739 as a violent storm raged in a dark purple sky over the Palace of Versailles. Her first cry coincided with a tremendous bolt of lightning followed immediately by a loud clap of thunder. The midwife's face creased with concern, it was considered to be a bad omen to give birth during a thunderstorm, as Odette, her eyes wide open, gripping the midwife's hand, struggled with the labour pains to bring her first child into the world.

No one watching Edouard as he stood outside the birthing chamber of his wife Odette, would know how much his emotions were churning over inside. His face impassive, he was thinking back to the death of his first wife after their second son, Nicholas had been born.

He then recalled how he had first met Odette at a ball here at the Palace.

Edouard, a thin, spare man, and one of the King's most important ministers, was still amazed that Odette had agreed to marry him. As a bright, vibrant young woman who enjoyed dancing so much, she could have had her pick of any of the young courtiers who vied for her attention, however she had agreed to marry him, a man who was well known for his devotion to the King and his duties.

His temperament was such that he didn't show much emotion except affection to his wife and children. However today, he subconsciously smoothed his wig several times and adjusted his beautifully embroidered waistcoat as he paced fretfully outside Odette's chamber.

The antechamber held some of the Ladies in Waiting to Queen Maria, Louis XVth Polish wife, who having given birth many times herself, was anxious to find out the progress of Odette, one of her favourite ladies in waiting. Odette held the post of a lady in waiting to the Queen, by virtue of being a distant family member to King Louis XV.

A few courtiers lingered in the corridor too, awaiting the results of the Odette's labour, having nothing better to do than to place bets on the sex of the Minister's first child to be born here.

Lost in his thoughts, Edouard wasn't aware that some of the ladies were admiring his rich clothing and his fine legs encased in white stockings above his buckled shoes.

Whilst waiting the outcome of events, drumming his fingers on the decorated wall panelling, Edouard thought too that he wasn't concerned if the child was a girl or a boy as long as Odette survived the ordeal of birth. He thought briefly of his two young sons, Armand and Nicolas now without their mother, living in the country with their mother's family, being brought up in the correct manner as befitted young gentlemen.

He thought too of Louis XV who had been delighted by his first born twin daughters after rumours and doubts that the King would not be able to father children at all.

He was brought back from his thoughts by the cry of his newborn child and waited impatiently for the midwife to inform him of the event. His feeling was one of relief when the midwife, still wearing her bloodied apron, eventually opened the heavy door and came out and curtsied to him. 'Your Grace, your Duchess is well and you have a healthy daughter.'

He allowed himself a small smile of relief as he thrust some coins into the midwife's hand before he hurried into Odette's darkened bed chamber, waving aside the consternation of her tending women as it was not customary for men to enter the birthing chamber.

As usual with the confinement of pregnant women, Odette's bedchamber was dark with religious tapestries hung over the windows to block out as much light from the outside world as possible. A large crucifix was evident there to provide spiritual support and only a single window was left open to allow fresh air into the room, as it was believed that too much light could damage the expectant mother's eyes.

Some of the Queen's other Ladies in Waiting now crowded around the door, straining to have a look at Odette and the newborn child, whilst one had slipped away to give the Queen the news that Odette had been delivered of a healthy daughter. Mathilde, Odette's closest friend, who was with the Queen was also anxiously waiting to hear the news about her dear friend and her first baby.

Odette had been moved from the birthing bed back into the large four poster bed and Edouard thought how Odette looked so small there, her blonde hair a little awry, her face wan and tired but she smiled at him timidly.

'My lord, I am so sorry', her lip quivered, 'a daughter, not a son.' He smiled kindly at her 'Do not worry, my sweet, I am the father of two sons already as you know and I am thankful to God that you have done well here today' kissing her gently on the forehead. 'We will call her Sophia after my mother.'

At least she had survived the birth Edouard thought, giving thanks to God, however he was aware that Odette still had to get through her entire recovery without infection.

Edouard then frowned as he realised that Odette's younger, headstrong sister, Adele, was absent from her sister's bedchamber. No doubt, he concluded to himself, up to her usual activities and intrigues with the other courtiers.

Edouard then looked at his new daughter, her face red and screwed up, as she continued to cry loudly in the midwife's arms, seemingly indignant at her arrival in the world. She was a robust baby who would continue to scream for the rest of the night. He watched as the midwife turned the baby over to the wet nurse as her weary mother fell asleep, blissfully unaware of what was yet to come with this child.

By contrast, Sophia's younger sister, Marie-Therese, born two years later, was delivered into the world on a calm day in late February, snow falling, quietly shrouding the countryside and the Palace in white.

Like the King, who favoured the second of his firstborn twins, Anne Henriette, Edouard doted on Marie-Therese who quickly became her father's favourite. She was a gentle, quiet child who suited his fastidious nature.

The Palace was noisy and crowded with thousands of people congregating there some days, all anxious to see the King or petition him and find their way into Court life if they could. One evening as Edouard left his office, soon after Marie-Therese was born, he found yet again people crowding the corridors, near the King's offices and apartments with the smells of some unwashed bodies and clothing apparent.

His face showing distaste, he held his richly embroidered bag of herbs and petals to his nose to disguise the smells of the place as he moved through the throng of people.

He heartily disliked the crowds and the lack of space and hygiene, however, his work as a Minister to the King demanded that he spent his days here.

Being particularly tired from his day at the High Council meeting discussing national and foreign policy with the King and other ministers of State, all he desired now was some peace and quiet with his own family.

From innate courtesy, Edouard consulted Odette that evening over dinner on moving their family into a rented house in the Versailles town, however his mind was already made up. Odette, had no problem with moving out of the Palace either although her reasons were entirely different from Edouard.

The behaviour at Court offended her religious beliefs greatly. She knew that the Court was rife with affairs and intrigues often where hedonistic and debauched behaviour was seen and seldom were married couples faithful to each other. So she was very pleased that Edouard had decided to move their family away from what she considered the depraved machinations of the Palace.

It didn't take Edouard long to procure a mansion with a garden encircled by a large wall for privacy only a short distance from the Palace. Odette took his face in her hands and kissed him when he told her of their new home. He was pleasantly surprised by Odette's reaction as he had not realised that moving meant so much to her.

Their days were long at the Palace, however Odette and Edouard both enjoyed returning to their new home to be with their children when their Palace duties were over for the day. They particularly liked the privacy of walking together in the neat gardens of their home in the evenings, where at present, pink and white blossom of the cherry trees bloomed overhead.

One evening, not long after moving in, they were sitting on a bench under the trees watching Sophia and Marie-Therese explore the garden. Sophia's interest in the garden was short lived, however little Marie-Therese looked closely at the flowers, picked one carefully and carried it over to her parents and placed it in her mother's lap.

'Oh look Edouard, she has picked a pink carnation. Do you know what that means?'

'No, my dearest, but I am sure you will tell me' he said smiling down at Odette but dismissing the meanings of flowers as a woman's fantasy. She smiled back at him 'It symbolises the love of a woman and a mother.'

Edouard raised an eyebrow 'How appropriate' he responded, picking up Marie-Therese and placing her on his lap and kissing her on the top of her head.

Marie-Therese looked up into her father's face saying 'Love you Papa' before climbing down and running off to where Sophia, who was laughing loudly, played with one of the nursemaids.

Mathilde and Odette had been close friends from childhood, growing up in the country together, but contrasted greatly in looks. Where Odette was petite and blonde, Mathilde was taller, dark haired, with a long face and darker complexion.

Today, as usual, Mathilde was wearing one of her many gowns of deep lilac, the colour she favoured, which Odette told her suited her so well. Odette had chosen a duck egg blue gown edged with white lace around the neckline and large bows at her elbows above the ruffled edge of her sleeves.

They had a free afternoon and Odette had invited Mathilde to come over to their house to see her children and sit in the garden as the weather was so beautiful. Whilst on their way back to the house, sitting together in a carriage, Mathilde had commented that she wondered if the weather at the times of Odette's children's births had affected their natures.

Sophia, born during a thunderstorm, was a fiery, impetuous girl, whereas her younger sister, Marie Therese, born during the quiet of falling snow, was a thoughtful,watchful child. Odette looked back at her friend, tilting her head to one side in thought.

'Well, Mathilde, that is an interesting thought. Sophia is so headstrong, like a force of nature and we don't know what to do with her. Discipline appears to have no effect on her. It just seems that she wants to win, no matter what the cost, whereas Marie-Therese, as you so well observe, is a much gentler child.'

Mathilde nodded her agreement at Odette's words, however, being unmarried herself, had no experienced answer for her friend as to how to deal with her lawless first child.

As the two friends entered the nursery, the governess and nursemaids dropped curtsies to them. The governess wore a harried look as yet again Sophia, at seven years old, was running amok, to the despair of her and the nursemaids. Dark ringlets and a green dress made Sophia a pretty picture but her behaviour running around the table and chairs and knocking into the rocking horse with her sturdy arms flailing and screaming as she did so, made her a most undesirable child.

Meanwhile by contrast, little Marie-Therese, at age five, was sitting quietly in the corner playing with blocks of wood with alphabet letters. She sat there building them up and taking them down to re-arrange them, occasionally looking up at her sister, as though studying her, while Sophia was causing such a fuss.

Odette shook her head at her firstborn, not knowing what to do or say to quieten her down except to offer her the box of sweetmeats she had brought with her. Sophia snatched the box from her mother, sitting down quickly on the floor by the day bed, scooping several sweets at once and stuffing them into her mouth. Mathilde knew better than to make a comment to her mother about Sophia's belligerent behaviour as she already knew that Odette was deeply concerned at Sophia's conduct.

Sophia, pacified with sweetmeats, was licking the sugar off her fingers. Looking up at her mother and the nursemaids, she had a smug look on her round face, as if she already knew she could always get the better of her elders with her boisterous ways.

Odette shook her head at Sophia as she and Mathilde moved over to her other daughter, their gowns swishing across the wooden floors.

Marie-Therese was picked up by one of the nursemaids so that her mother could talk to her. 'Hello, my little one' Odette said, fondling her daughter's blonde curly hair, smiling at her and thinking how sweet and docile she was by contrast to her older sister.

Standing next to Odette and looking down, Mathilde saw to her horror that the alphabet bricks that Marie-Therese had being playing with, were now arranged to spell out the word 'curse'.

Mathilde, putting her hand to her mouth and turning away from Odette, recalled a recent event which occurred when Odette had been leaving the palace in her carriage.

Beggars had, as usual, crowded around the fine carriage, begging for money, however on this occasion, Odette had had no money with her to give to them.

One of the older ladies, dirty, care worn and dressed in rags, had shouted at Odette that she may keep her money but her family would be cursed with unhappiness.

The beggar's face, dark with anger as she waved her fist in the air, had frightened Odette so much, had sworn to her friend that she would always have money ready for the beggars in the future.

As Odette moved away from her younger daughter, Mathilde looked at Marie-Therese and noticed her intense stare, her large blue eyes looking at her mother's back.

'Child', she asked 'Why are you looking at your mother like that?' however Marie-Therese didn't have the words to describe the shadows she saw around her mother.

Not long after their visit to the nursery, Odette became unwell.

Chapter 2

Louis' wife, Queen Marie, was of a quiet, pious disposition who spent a great deal of her time with her Polish countrymen in her own court, playing music, reading her Bible and playing cards. She did, however, have a great interest in music so every Sunday, the Queen would arrange concerts at Court which became an important part of the life at Versailles.

Odette and Mathilde felt for this shy, nervous woman, and had seen that the King and Queen being devoted to each other in their early marriage. Their similar temperaments had given them a preference for enjoying intimate suppers together with less rigid etiquette and events that were out of the public eye.

Subsequently, though they discussed how sad it was for the Queen as she was now shunned by the King.

The Queen, having produced ten children, almost dying giving birth to Princess Louise in 1737 and having a stillborn child the following year, had been advised by her doctors to have a break from pregnancies.

As a result, she subsequently refused Louis entrance to her bedchamber.

Louis had taken great offence at her actions and was so angry that he never shared her bed after that, now only meeting with her for necessary ceremonies and Court events.

Odette and Mathilde also thought how difficult it must be for the Queen to go through the humiliating custom of being introduced to the King's latest mistress in full view of the Court as well as to her introduction to the rest of the royal family.

It was the Court custom that dictated that this etiquette was required of the new mistress in order for her to stay and participate in Court life, which all seemed grossly wrong to Odette.

Odette was sure that she couldn't have performed so perfectly either, looking at Queen Marie's passive face at the time of Marquise de Pompadour's introduction the year before. No one could guess the Queen's true feelings on the matter.

One of the Queen's great pleasures though was to serve her waiting ladies herself with the new rare and expensive drink of hot spicy chocolate from Mexico. The Queen took delight in the ceremony using the porcelain and silver tea service she had received as a gift on the birth of the Dauphin.

One late afternoon, as the sun was setting casting long shadows into the Queen's salon, Odette and Mathilde were enjoying drinking hot chocolate with Queen Marie. When they had finished, they received confirmation from her that they could now leave her chambers as their duties were over for the day. They both curtsied and the Queen waved her hand in dismissal, her thoughts already on other matters.

As they moved through the Queen's antechambers, Odette turned to her friend, suddenly sitting down heavily in a blue brocade chair, fanning herself with her beautifully decorated fan. 'Oh Mathilde, I can't believe how hot and tired I feel, and I keep coughing.'

Mathilde looked at Odette's very pale face and seeing one of the younger ladies in waiting, Celeste, passing by, she instructed her to bring Odette a glass of wine quickly.

Mathilde, having observed Celeste's slender yellow dressed figure, her smiling dark eyes, and her fresh young face under burnished oak coloured hair, thought that she would be one to catch the eye of the King sooner or later.

Odette coughed again and her eyes opened in horror as she noticed spots of blood on her white handkerchief. She plucked nervously at her gold and pearl necklace saying 'Oh God, help me!'

Whatever is it, my dear?' she said, turning back to Odette surprised at her outburst.

Odette offered up her handkerchief and Mathilde's eyes widened in horror. Mathilde knew at once what was troubling Odette, coughing up blood like this was a sign of the fatal disease, consumption.

Odette was put to bed by her ladies that late afternoon, never to leave her chambers again. As the days turned into weeks, Odette started to fail. Coughing, sweats and chills plagued her, the disease spreading to her organs as she began to waste away.

Edouard was beside himself, spending as much time as he could at her bedside, imploring the doctors to do something, anything to save his beloved Odette. Mathilde sat with her too, holding her hand, feeling such empathy and grief for her oldest friend, knowing what was to come.

Mathilde had spent many hours sitting in Odette's bedchamber, reminiscing with her over their lives together but now Odette no longer had the energy to talk and often slept. Mathilde both admired and was glad of Odette's strong faith, as she herself wasn't so sure of her beliefs about the heavenly afterlife.

A few days later, when Odette finally lay dying, she told Mathilde that she wanted her younger sister, Adele, to come to her bedside so she could give her instructions in supervising Sophia and Marie-Therese's upbringing.

Edouard and Mathilde agreed that it was also time to call the priest to come to give Odette the last rites and he arrived within the hour having received the urgent message to come to the house.

The priest, in his dark robes with a kindly face, came into the room and stepped forward to the bed. He leaned over Odette anointing her forehead with oil in the shape of a cross saying 'Through this holy anointing, may the Lord in his love and mercy help you with the grace of the Holy Spirit. May the Lord who frees you from sin save you and raise you up.'

Odette smiled at him briefly after he had finished speaking.

The priest, having performed his service, quietly left having said to Edouard that he would now go and pray for Odette's soul.

After some time, with Edouard checking the clock anxiously, he heard a carriage come to a stop outside their house. Adele had finally arrived and swept into the bedchamber having given her coat and hat to the manservant in the hall below. Today, she was dressed in a light green dress with a low cut square neckline and tight bodice, exhibiting her full bosom, adorned with ribbons, and a fine pearl necklace around her neck which caught the light of the candles in the room.

Adele appeared not to notice Odette's frailty as she sat on the chair next to the bed arranging her skirts before looking at her older sister.

Odette licked her lips and Mathilde moved quickly across the bedchamber to give Odette a drink before she started to talk.

Odette then looked up into her sister's face saying with difficulty 'Please help Edouard with my girls as he is so involved with the King duties'. She paused to get her breath 'They will need instruction from a lady on how to grow up and please, I beg of you, ensure that they have sufficient religious education' she broke off, coughing again.

Adele stayed back, anxious not to become infected by her sister's malady fingering her pearl necklace absently.

Odette who thought the best of everyone had no idea of Adele's actual thoughts.

Mathilde looked on with pity at her friend, as she joined Adele at the beside, taking Odette's frail hand in hers as Odette whispered her final instructions to Adele. Her sister looked at her, nodding in agreement with everything she was saying and once she had finished speaking, Odette closed her eyes for the final time.

Mathilde heard Edouard make a choking sound as he came forward and knelt by Odette's bed, laying his head next to hers on the pillow tears streaming down his face.

Several female servants stood by patiently waiting in the shadows of the large room, to make the necessary arrangements of the laying out of Odette's body.

One of the younger servants was crying as she watched the scene in the bedchamber. Odette had been particularly kind to her when she had first arrived. Overwhelmed by the Palace and its people, Odette had moved her to their house. One of the older servants pinched the young girl's arm as a warning against this display of emotion in front of her betters.

Standing next to the bed, Mathilde, her face wet with tears, looked at Adele whose hard face showed no sign of grief at her sister's demise.

Mathilde, unhappily, did not believe a word of the agreement Adele had just made to her sister regarding her nieces welfare.

Mathilde knew very well that Court life did little to help with moral codes, despite the very rigid code of etiquette that people had to follow, as the King himself had his mistresses and illegitimate children.

It was no wonder, she thought, as the courtiers lived such dissolute lives. With Adele as one of its primary activists, she would do little in the way of spiritual guidance for her nieces.

Much later, Mathilde sadly realised that she was proved absolutely right about Adele's character too. She had watched in disbelief, over the following months, as Adele, a widow from her marriage to an elderly husband, tried to persuade the grieving Edouard to marry her, saying how she could look after him and his girls.

Mathilde, however knew that Adele's real motives for trying to marry Edouard was because she badly needed his money to cover her heavy gambling debts and enormous dress making bills.

Mathilde worried endlessly over whether to say anything to Edouard about Adele. However, in the end, felt it just wasn't her place to say anything as she didn't really have any proof, but her instincts told her she was correct.

She badly missed her friend, Odette, who always had a smile ready and a kind word for anyone she felt needed help and none of this would he happening if only she were still alive. Edouard was too bereft to even acknowledge Adele's advances and Mathilde was supremely grateful when Adele tired of the chase and looked around the Court for better game than the grieving brother in law.

Mathilde also saw Adele ignore everything she had promised her sister about guiding her nieces in their religious studies, instead she manipulated them, particularly Sophia when she was much older, for her own ends with her licentious Court intrigues.

No one yet knew of the calamitous events that were to follow.

Chapter 3

12 years later
Versailles 1758

Marie-Therese lingered in the Hall of Mirrors looking through the window at the elaborate gardens from the Water Parterre stretching away towards the horizon. The sun was shining, birds were singing and the grounds were taking on the new growth of Spring. It was a season that Marie-Therese particularly loved after the hard cold days of winter.

It was just past her birthday and at seventeen, she was a beauty to behold: blonde and blue eyed like her mother Odette, she had a slim build and graceful carriage. She wore a dark blue gown, her favourite colour, adorned with pearls which accentuated her colouring looking dramatic against her pale skin and blonde hair.

She had a natural humility and seemed completely unaware of the looks that came her way from the young male members of the Court. Of course, being the daughter of the one of the King's ministers did nothing to detract from her appeal either as others were always keen to advance themselves by becoming her ally or possibly her husband.

Today, as she looked out at the gardens, she was in deep thought, thinking about something she had seen one evening recently. Walking through the Palace corridors back to her rooms, she had turned a corner and seen a courtier, in an alcove, taking advantage of a young serving girl. Then, having finished with her, he had thrown a coin on the floor at her feet as payment.

With her innate sense of justice, she pondered on why some people could get away with such behaviour without consequences. She wished others would have more compassion and be less self absorbed as they carried on a life of debauchery in all their finery.

She realised that she was finding it more and more difficult to cope with some of the conduct at the Court, not least that of her aunt and sister. No one seemed faithful to their partners and many contrived and manipulated others in order to get closer to the King and enjoy the advantages that would bring them.

She now recalled a conversation a few weeks ago when she had been visiting with her mother's old close friend, Mathilde, who was now retired as her sight was failing. They had sat in the small dark drawing room of Mathilde's home near the Palace and Mathilde's only devoted servant had served them coffee and small cakes.

Mathilde, who loved to talk as she had so few visitors, had been reminiscing about when the

King and the Polish twenty one year old Marie Leszczyńska were first married and how devoted they had been to each other before the days of the King taking mistresses.

Mathilde went on to describe his first mistress, Louise Julie de Mailly who was from a noble family and the King had made her a Duchess.

Mathilde talked for a while of the mistresses and illegitimate children of the King and particularly of Jeanne-Antoinette Poisson, promoted by Louis as he given her the title of the Marquise de Pompadour.

Mathilde continued that the Court had been shocked when the King took this mistress from the lower classes, but she surprised everyone by lasting for so long, initially as his mistress, but now as his long term friend.

Marie-Therese listened as Mathilde recalled the old story of the Marquise de Pompadour's rise to fame. How at nine years old, it had been predicted by a soothsayer that she would reign over the King's heart. She had consequently been groomed by family members in the ways of Court etiquette for when she met the King and to fulfil her destiny as had been told to her years ago.

And so it came about that she was an indispensable comfort to Louis XV, captivating and amusing him with elegant parties, hunting and journeying between the King's estates.

Mathilde had commented that at least the Marquise de Pompadour had been kind to the Queen, even getting Louis to upgrade the Queen's apartments, although Mathilde, like Odette had, disapproved of the Marquise's mode of living otherwise.

The Marquise had had several miscarriages and frail health, Mathilde continued, so now she refrained from being in Louis' bed without the disastrous results that the Queen now endured.

The Marquise was a clever woman who not only organised entertainments to uplift Louis from his melancholic moods, but also arranged for a string of nubile and not very intellectual young women to satisfy Louis' appetites in the bedchamber.

Now, as Maria-Therese stood deep in thought about the conduct of the King and his court, she was unaware of the approach of two of the courtiers.

Two young men sauntered along the Hall of Mirrors, best of friends but very different in character and looks. One tall and slim with dark eyes, Sebastian, and the other, Gabriel, more of a stocky build, with blue eyes.

Sebastian, well aware of his good looks and

tall build, was an adventurer, reckless to a fault whereas his friend, Gabriel was possessed of a more thoughtful and studious nature. Gabriel enjoyed gambling as much as Sebastian but wasn't quite the philanderer like him.

Gabriel was Marie-Therese's father's protege and they had met many times since Gabriel had started working with her father.

Gabriel very much desired Marie-Therese and was pleased to come across her in the busy Palace where he may not have seen her for days otherwise.

Gabriel nudged Sebastian, who grinned knowingly back at his friend. Sebastian had to admit that Marie-Therese was very enticing, someone he would have enjoyed teaching the etiquette of lovemaking if she were not the object of his friend's affection.

Gabriel greeted her, bowing and sweeping his feathered cap in front on her. She looked up as his arrival, brought her out of her pensive reverie. She shook her head briefly, smiling, taking in his dark blue eyes, his kind smile, his beautifully made clothes and immaculate white wig.

He smiled back at her, taking in her beauty which made him want her so very much. He thought briefly of the difference between Marie Therese and her sister Sophia, with such different looks and characters. He could see depths in Marie-

Therese eyes where there was a kindness which was entirely lacking in Sophia.

Almost as if he had conjured her up, Sophia rushed up to the group now, a whirlwind with her dark curls bouncing on her shoulders above her shimmering green dress, quickly insinuating herself between Gabriel and her sister.

'Come, come,' she ordered Marie Therese, 'Aunt Adele has been made Mistress of the Revels and is arranging a masked ball and wants our help and of course, we will need new dresses for the occasion' she babbled on excitedly, taking Marie-Therese's hand and pulling her away from Gabriel.

Sophia flashed a disarming smile at Sebastian, who was standing next to Gabriel, knowing full well that he desired her.

Sophia, more voluptuous than Marie-Therese twirled around her sister, her low cut emerald dress showing her high bosom. She stepped towards Sebastian and managed to brush against him before she danced away pulling Marie-Therese with her. She loved to tease him but had no wish to become one of his many conquests.

She then artfully smiled back at Gabriel, fully aware of his feelings for her sister, saying 'I will make it up to you' the dimples showing in her smooth cheeks. Little did Marie-Therese know how Sophia would do that.

Dutifully, Marie-Therese followed her sister out of the gallery throwing an apologetic look at Gabriel, as she was aware of his interest in her. In a recent conversation she had had with her father, he mentioned how pleased he was with Gabriel's work and conduct at Court which made her feel that maybe he was someone with whom she could have a common interest.

Chapter 4

Later that day, Sophia, sitting at her dressing table adjusting her dark curls, was thinking what her aunt Adele had told her about seducing men.

Most men, Adele had taught her, were interested in themselves first and after that, they just wanted to bed as many women as possible, so manipulate them first, and use them to your advantage.

She continued that the way to treat men was much like training pets. When they did something you wanted them to do, reward them with a treat: a meaningful smile, a touch, or a flash of an ankle and that made them want to do more for you. Praise and reward them if they did well but punish them if they didn't. Sophia had seen her aunt drop certain acquaintances when they displeased her, and then seen these men go to great lengths to get back into her good books.

Use or be used: this was her aunt's creed.

Whilst thinking this through, Sophia tilted her head one way and then another checking that she looked perfect. She admired her alabaster skin and her dark eyes with long eyelashes and the small mole on her cheek. She didn't have to make a beauty spot that was so fashionable, she was already beautifully made she decided.

A thought crossed her mind about Sebastian and Gabriel. She wasn't prepared to give in to Sebastian yet but wondered whether she could prise Gabriel from his adoration of her sister, especially as she had promised she would make it up to him after taking Marie-Therese away the other day.

Having nothing to hold her attention at present, she laughed and set herself the challenge; thinking of her strategy to get Gabriel into her bed while keeping Sebastian at arm's length, as she refused to be like one of the other silly girls who just fell instantly under his charm.

It didn't take long for Sophia to achieve her aim. A few days later, she waited in one of the rooms near her father's office for Gabriel to finish his work, playing cards with her friends. The clock had just struck 6 pm when he finally exited her father's office and walked through the room where she was, on his way back to his own chambers.

When Sophia saw him, she quickly threw down her cards to the consternation of the other players and moved away from the table. She fell in step with him, as he hurried on, his arms full of books, looking harried.

'Hello Gabriel, are you all right?' she queried innocently.

'Oh, hello, it's nothing really,' Gabriel replied impatiently 'just a lot of work to do as the King has just decided on a new building project.'

Sophia touched his arm 'Slow down and relax a little. Here let us stop and sit on this window seat for a moment.' Gabriel smiled back at her. He heaved a sigh, 'Yes, what a good idea, I just get so busy, I forget to stop' he replied, piling the books onto the seat and sitting back, stretching out his long legs in front of him.

Sophia took in his good looks and found herself very much in favour of her devious plan. She stopped a passing servant and demanded wine to be served to them immediately. The girl curtsied quickly and rushed away to do Sophia's bidding.

The wine arrived and putting the goblet to his lips, Gabriel was surprised to find he was enjoying Sophia's solicitous company, whereas in the past he had always found her to be so self centered, always wanting to be the centre of attention.

While they were drinking together, Sophia asked intelligent questions getting Gabriel to talk on subjects she knew he enjoyed. She knew that one of Gabriel's interests was astronomy which he learned from the King. Gabriel talked at length about the King's new building projects and the economics involved.

Sophia hid her boredom well. And was careful

not to drink as much as Gabriel, but often topped up his glass. She watched as Gabriel became intoxicated. She knew he had had a hard night of drinking with Sebastian the night before and it didn't help that she had skillfully added a tincture of something to his glass, without him noticing, which her aunt often used to get others to comply with her wishes.

As the sun began to set, and the shadows lengthened in the gardens she feigned tiredness and asked sweetly whether Gabriel could escort her back to her rooms.

Gabriel, being the gentleman he was, did as he was asked, belatedly remembering to pick up his books. Walking unsteadily, he took Sophia to her chambers.

As they entered Sophia's bedroom, her King Charles spaniel puppy, a birthday gift from Marie-Therese, jumped up at her excitedly, clawing at her skirts. Sophia pushed him away, irritated, as always, by his demands for her attention.

Without demur, Gabriel sat down hard on the stool by the fireplace, 'That wine seems unusually strong' he murmured, running his hand over his forehead. 'Come' Sophia's said, 'A little more can't hurt'.

As Gabriel didn't reply, she poured them more wine and suggested that Gabriel lie down on her bed as he appeared tired.

Gabriel looked up wearily at her, 'No, no I must go and start on the King's instructions before the evening is over'.

Sophia took no notice and with her soft hands, she pulled him to his feet guiding him onto the sumptuous purple covers of her four poster bed.

Gently, she started to undo his clothes, whispering that he could relax better without them. She undid the gold buttons to his silk coat and waistcoat. With his eyes half closed, he allowed her to do as she suggested. She smiled to herself as the light of the fire showed his face relaxing.

Before he knew it, she was beside him on the bed, running her fingers over his body and under his shirt. He opened his eyes wide and he turned to her, taking her in his arms, his long stifled passion for Marie-Therese taking over.

After their lovemaking, Sophia smiled triumphantly in the dark as they lay in the tangled sheets. He quickly fell asleep, his head resting on her bosom and Sophia thought how easy it was, as always, to get her own way.

There was a knock at the door, and without thinking, Sophia called out for the caller to come in, expecting it to be her maid to get her ready before she went to supper with her Aunt Adele.

They always talked about their various conquests and as she lay in bed with Gabriel, she thought how much she would enjoy sharing this experience with her aunt.

The candles in the room flickered as the door opened, the fire throwing shadows around the room. Marie-Therese stepped into the room and seeing Sophia sitting up in bed, moved closer 'Are you unwell, Sophia?' she asked with concern in her voice.

The dark curtain tied around the bedpost had obscured part of the bed, so at first Marie-Therese didn't see anyone but Sophia, however as she drew closer, she saw Gabriel in her sister's arms, his eyes closed. She stepped back, her hand across her mouth, mouthing, 'oh, no, no, no' before running from the room in distress.

Her friends waiting outside of Sophia's chambers for Maria-Therese were astonished at the change in her demeanour. She rushed past them before pausing along the corridor, trying to control her sobs, her chest heaving, banging her fist impotently against a marble statue after what she had just seen.

Sebastian was a little way away down the corridor, looking for his friend Gabriel, when he came across the group of young women huddled together with an air of consternation. He recognised them as Marie-Therese friends, so pausing in his search for Gabriel, he strode over to find out what was causing the commotion.

He found Marie-Therese in a heap on the floor in the centre of the group. One of her close friends looking frightened and said to Sebastian 'We don't know what the matter is, she has just fainted. Something in her sister's room upset her I think.' He looked down at Marie-Therese, seeing her eyelids fluttering as she returned to consciousness.

Marie-Therese looked up at him, her pale face covered in tears. 'Gabriel and Sophia in bed together' she uttered, gesturing with one of her arms towards Sophia's rooms.

'Get her back to her rooms and get her servants to look after her' he instructed. The women did as he said, getting Marie-Therese to feet   and together supporting Marie-Therese, they took away.

Afterwards he paced the floor wondering why his friend, who had long held a passion for Marie-Therese had gone to Sophia's bed instead.

He remembered he had smiled indulgently at Gabriel when he talked recently of summoning up the courage to ask her father for Marie-Therese's hand in marriage.

'There is plenty of time for that' was his response, 'Look at all the fun that can be had here' waving his arm at the crowded court where many women, beautifully dressed and beguiling, were waiting for some attention. Gabriel, however, could not be dissuaded from his course of action concerning Marie-Therese.

Sebastian was very angry with Sophia as he felt sure she had seduced Gabriel for her own pleasure. Sophia was a prize that he wanted for himself and she had cleverly eluded him for a very long time.

He had seen her at work, going after certain men, manipulating them for her own ends but keeping him at arm's length.

The more he thought about it, the angrier he got. He returned to his own chambers, calling to his valet for wine, while he sat in front of the fire deciding what he was going to do about Sophia.

She flirted with him constantly but always kept him away. In fact, sometimes he even thought about her while other women were in his bed.

He wanted to beat her, subdue her to his will, but knowing that she was a very intelligent woman who could get the better of most people he knew, he wasn't sure how to handle her or this situation. He could reach no conclusion but vowed that once the night was through he would find some way to deal with Sophia's antics.

He sought out Gabriel early the next morning in his rooms and found him nursing a hangover, looking very pale. He then told Sebastian what had happened the previous evening.

He continued before Sebastian could speak, looking dejectedly at his friend saying 'I swear to God, that witch, Sophia did something to me, I never had a chance. I never meant this to happen, you have to believe me, I love Marie-Therese, you know I do. Sophia told me she put something in my drink and laughed in my face before I left' his voice petering out as he ran out of words to describe his despair.

He was in a terrible state, regretting deeply what had happened and went paler still when Sebastian told him 'Oh Gabriel it is worse than you fear, I came across Marie-Therese leaving Sophia's room last night having seen you together.'

Gabriel literally reeled back in shock. Sebastian thought his friend looked near collapse and pushed him onto the window seat. Gabriel struggled with him 'No, no, I must go to Marie-Therese and explain.'

'No' Sebastian said 'You told me Edouard is seeing the King today about his new building project and you have to be there too'. Gabriel now remembering the King's instructions looked wretchedly at him.

'Leave this with me, Gabriel. You had better go

to work and I will try and sort it out. I will go and see how Marie-Therese is doing and talk with her. Go', he urged his friend, who stood up wearily to make his way towards Edouard's offices, dragging his feet, his heart heavy and steps slow, his body stooped over as he walked out of his room.

Seeing how his friend was suffering, Sebastian's anger was re-ignited and he swore to himself that he would get even with Sophia not knowing that he would be setting off another trail of events that would be disastrous.

He strode about the wing of the palace where their rooms were situated, his anger mounting all the time, his thoughts scattered. He walked backwards and forwards outside of Sophia's room wondering what he could say to her.

The antechamber room opened as a servant left and he heard Sophia's distinctive laugh from within which angered him still further. Without consent, he strode through the antechamber into her bed chamber seeing her dressed in just her chemise, as she was a habitual late riser, with another servant combing her hair. 'Get out' he bellowed to the young girl, who scampered away, terrified at his belligerent manner.

'What is this about Sebastian?' Sophia enquired coolly of him as she stood up, not the least embarrassed that she wasn't dressed appropriately for visitors.

'Sebastian plunged forward, his face red and his arms shaking. 'You evil little piece of work, I know about you and Gabriel' he shouted.

Sophia stepped back alarmed at his manner. Sebastian grabbed hold of her and threw her on the rumpled bed. 'You think you are above me, and you can manipulate and harm my friends, do you?'

He climbed onto the bed, pulling up her shift as he did so. 'I am going to make you pay for what you have done' he hissed at her.

For the first time in her life, Sophia was really scared. She always had control of her life before but this was terrifying. She screamed out loud as one of his hands crushed her breasts as he fumbled to open his breeches with the other.

Adele, approaching Sophia's room was surprised to see Sophia's maid rush out of the door. She caught her on the arm and demanded to know what was going on before she heard Sophia's loud screaming. She released her grip on the girl's arm, rushed past her and ran through the room to Sophia's bedchamber.

Adele's nostrils flared as she saw the scene before her. Sebastian holding Sophia down on the bed with her shift pushed up exposing her long pale legs that she was try to kick at Sebastian. Looking down at Sophia, he saw her look away from him, her eyes wide.

Sebastian suddenly became aware of someone else in the room and looking over his shoulder. He saw Adele advancing on him, her face screwed up in anger. She reached into her petticoat pocket withdrawing a small dagger she kept there for her own protection. She lunged at Sebastian catching him on the shoulder as he turned to her, missing his back which is where she had intended to plunge her dagger.

Sebastian got up quickly cursing at her holding his bleeding shoulder. 'You witch, you are responsible for what your niece gets up to.'

'How dare you try to take her without her permission,' Adele shot back.

Sophia had stumbled off the bed and collapsed on a red chaise-longue near her dressing table looking very pale.

'Oh don't give me that,' he shouted back at Adele, 'you are as coldhearted as her,' gesturing at Sophia 'and what is really upsetting you is that I won't take you to my bed, because you are too old for me.'

Adele, her normally impassive face now a mask of anger, blustered 'That is not true' but they all knew that it was.

Mortified, Adele screamed at him 'Get out, I will make you pay for your actions' hating the young twenty five year old philanderer for speaking the truth. For years she had been able to seduce any man she wanted, young or old, but now, at nearly forty years old, was not meeting with quite as much of her previous successes.

Sebastian quickly weighed his options, realising that Adele could do him more damage unless he left rapidly. He curled his lip at her in disgust as he made his way out of Sophia's bedchamber holding his bleeding shoulder.

Adele dropping her dagger, rushing to lock the door before going over to her niece and putting a wrap around her shoulders. 'Don't you worry, my love, I will get even with him for what has happened here today.' Sophia, still shaking, laid her head on her aunt's shoulder, her confidence slowly returning as they discussed what to do next.

Chapter 5

Later that day, Sebastian stood next to Marie-Therese, his superficial wound in his shoulder now bandaged and hidden beneath his new green coat.

Her face was sad and her eyes red from crying. He took hold of her hands and pulled her down onto the seat as he knelt in front of her.

'Please forgive Gabriel, he is in a terrible state and I am afraid it was your sister who is more responsible for Gabriel ending up in her bedchamber.'

'Well, where is Gabriel?' she sniffed delicately into her lace edged handkerchief.

'Gabriel couldn't come to you himself, he and your father had work to do with the King today' Sebastian replied.

Haltingly, Marie-Therese whispered 'I know my sister and her character and my aunt is just as bad, but I never envisaged this happening. I don't think I can speak to either of them again or Gabriel for that matter.'

'For the love of God, give Gabriel a chance, please' Sebastian exhorted. 'Promise me that you will at least listen to his side of the story, your sister got him drunk and put something in his drink too. He told me Sophia had laughed in his face about it.'

Sebastian thought he saw a brief flash of light in Marie-Therese's eyes but it faded just as quickly. 'How can I ever trust him again?' she said as tears flowed down her cheeks.

Much later that afternoon, free from work, Gabriel approached Marie-Therese standing by the fireplace in one of the meeting rooms near the Hall of Mirrors. She looked pale but in control of herself, her russet coloured gown giving some warmth to her beautiful face.

He rushed to her side not caring that they were in a public place and looked imploring at her. 'Forgive me, please otherwise I will never be able to forgive myself for what has happened.'

Marie-Therese looked at him, his face contorted with emotion, 'Oh Gabriel, I cannot trust anyone here anymore, you, my sister or my aunt. I hate it, I hate it. This place is full of evil, I don't think I want to be here anymore' as she held her handkerchief to her lips.

He chewed his lip anxiously as he tried to think of something else to say to her but felt he could no longer reach her, as though a wall had come down between them.

She shook her head and moved away from him Feeling nothing would change, she wondered where the dark activities of her aunt and sister would take them.

Her sombre thoughts were that no good would come of this life in the Palace. Peoples actions didn't appear to have consequences as she observed the licentious life around her.

Her sister's ultimate betrayal had crystallized her feelings about the Court, that there was nothing good in it.

'Please, please give me some time to make it up to you' Gabriel pleaded with her, 'anything, anything' his voice faltering as he looked at her sad face.

'Oh Gabriel, I can't think clearly at the moment, maybe we can talk again another time' Marie-Therese said as she looked at his pale face before walking away. She wanted to forgive Gabriel and to hug him but her emotions were in too much of a turmoil for her to think clearly.

As Adele had promised Sophia, she would get back at Sebastian for trying to rape her. Adele knew the King and the Marquise de Pompadour would be taking a walk in the Palace gardens in the afternoon as the King was always keen to share his hobby of botany with her.

Adele had a network of spies who kept her informed of the many necessary things she needed to know to make her activities work.

She placed herself in the grounds as she knew this was the route the King would take through the Rockwork Grove before stopping by the Fountain of Autumn where the gilt leaded statue of Bacchus was displayed with his harvest of grapes.

The musicians struck up music as the King's party approached. Adele had dressed in her most eye catching golden dress whose diamond decorations sparkled as they caught the sunlight.

As the party got nearer, Adele swept a deep curtsy. She despised the Marquise de Pompadour as she considered her to be in a lower class than herself, however, it was not politic for her to let the King know her feelings on his once mistress, now his long term friend. Adele should have been more grateful to the Marquise de Pompadour who arranged for Louis to be surrounded by witty and amusing people of whom Adele was one. He had given Adele the role and title of the Mistress of the Revels, responsible for organising games, dances and plays for the Court.

Adele didn't look up at Louis and kept her expression demure. The King looked at her with some surprise as she was normally entertaining and vivacious. 'Marquise de Volanges, does something ail you today?' he enquired, calling her by her married name even though she was widowed. 'Nothing is wrong, Sire' Adele responded quietly. 'Oh come, I know you better than that' he said. 'I demand you tell me what ails you'.

Maria-Therese had come into the gardens at that moment to deliver a note to her aunt from one of her aunt's latest lovers. She couldn't believe what she was seeing as her aunt playacted her part beautifully.

She listened in horror as she heard Adele embellish and lie about what had actually happened between Sebastian and Sophia. Marie-Therese had heard the servants gossip about the incident in Sophia's rooms with Adele and Sebastian and therefore knew what really had happened.

Adele, holding her hand to her full cleavage for effect, told the King of Sebastian entering Sophia's apartments and then raping her, her face a picture of distasteful emotion. She carefully omitted Sophia's behaviour with Gabriel as the cause of Sebastian confronting Sophia, and of herself stabbing Sebastian.

Marie-Therese saw the King's face grow angry at the story and she turned away in distress as she knew that things would not end well for Sebastian with the deceitfulness of her aunt's story. As the King moved away, she looked at Adele whose face now held a triumphant expression as she knew she had ruined Sebastian's reputation forever.

They all knew that the Court lived under the strict surveillance of the King and that the courtiers' careers depended on their strict observance of Court etiquette. So what Adele had told the King meant that Sebastian was now disgraced. The King would no longer acknowledge him and he would automatically be expelled from the Court.

Early the next morning a servant brought the letter to Sebastian's apartments as he was getting dressed for the day. He was busy admiring his new scarlet coat over his vest of gold satin in the mirror as his valet entered bearing the letter on a platter. He felt a stab of panic and a deep sense of foreboding as he took the letter from the platter recognising it as a missive from the King. He had known all along, deep down that Adele would have her revenge.

He went pale as he read the contents of his letter telling he was no longer required at Court and would have to return to his father's estates in the Loire.

As he saw the King's signature at the bottom of the letter, he collapsed on his unmade bed as he realised his career at Versailles had been destroyed for ever by Adele.

Chapter 6

The musicians played their instruments heralding the start of the Court's evening entertainment.

Little did anyone know that this was the last time the Court would see Adele as she cut a swathe through the courtiers and sashayed across the room, her brilliant peacock blue dress, the diamonds reflecting in the mirrors and the candlelight, her hand resting on the arm of her latest beau. Adele, Mistress of the Revels, had arrived to entertain King Louis and the Marquise de Pompadour.

She curtsied low as she reached the couple sitting in their elaborate chairs, before nodding to the group of musicians nearby to start the music to accompany her in one of her own witty and entertaining songs for which she was famous for throughout the Court.

She felt great satisfaction as the King laughed and applauded her afterwards saying 'You entertain us well, Marquise de Volanges'. Louis patted the Marquise's arm acknowledging that once again, she was responsible for this entertainment which lifted him out of melancholy.

Adele swept him a low curtsey displaying her ample bosom, covered with strands of pearl necklaces, smiling at the King's compliment, ignoring the fact that the Marquise de Pompadour was clapping her hands too.

Sebastian and Gabriel had spent hours together going over what Adele had done and the King's letter of dismissal. Sebastian was in despair and there was nothing that Gabriel could say or do to alleviate his friend's depression.

Together they packed up Sebastian's belongings before a sad farewell at the Palace gates. Sebastian's last words to Gabriel were 'This matter isn't over yet believe me, I will get that wicked witch for what she has done to me' as he climbed onto his favourite horse.

Gabriel couldn't have imagined what was yet to follow as he waved a farewell to Sebastian before turning towards the Palace to resume his duties.

He felt that the events were spiraling out of control, making him feel dispirited, feeling that there was nothing good about his life now.

Sebastian sent his luggage on to his father's estates, however he did not go straight home but rode his horse instead to a lowly Paris boarding house. He rented a small upstairs room from the bent backed and shabbily dressed owner.

The proprietor looked appraisingly at Sebastian and if he felt surprise at someone of Sebastian's aristocratic bearing and dress wanting a room he didn't show it, however his eyes gleamed with pleasure as Sebastian dropped some coins in his hand.

Sebastian climbed the stairs, looked around the cramped room with its low ceiling and small grubby window overlooking the noisy and smelly street. He found it distasteful after what he had been used to in Versailles but reconciled himself to the fact that he wouldn't be here long. He had also purchased some grubby clothing from the proprietor and now donned them quickly before walking out down the crowded streets to collect his horse to ride back to Versailles Palace.

For the last few days Sebastian, disguised as a beggar, had been waiting outside the Palace gates watching the procession of carriages leaving and returning to the Palace as the courtiers went about their daily activities of amusing the King. Sebastian bent his head low as he saw the King and the Marquise de Pompadour leave that morning and then, at last, he saw the carriage he had been waiting for: Adele was leaving the Palace to join the King at the hunting lodge where he was being entertained by the Marquise de Pompadour.

He had been waiting impatiently for Adele to leave the Palace to enable him to put his plan into action.

He saw Adele at the carriage window, beautifully dressed with her large hat with feathers, throwing coins to the beggars. Sebastian too had heard Odette's story of being cursed by the beggars for not giving out money and that Adele, despite her scheming ways, was at heart superstitious too therefore keen to prevent being cursed herself.

Sebastian manoeuvred his way through the mob and with a quick motion withdrew his pistol and aimed it at Adele.

The young driver of the carriage was already having problems as one of the horses was skittish with the beggars crowding around the carriage and hearing the pistol shot, the horse now bolted.

Sebastian quickly hid the pistol in his coat, bending down with the other beggars to conceal himself as he pretended to collect some of the coins that Adele had thrown them. If someone had observed him closely they would have seen that his face and hands were too clean and his clothing was not threadbare enough to be a regular beggar at the Palace gates. By the time the driver had regained control of the carriage, it was some distance from the palace gates. He pulled the horses to a stop as he leapt down to check on his passenger, fearful of the consequences of not controlling his horses and the carriage properly.

As he looked into the carriage he saw a scene

he didn't believe at first. Horrified, he saw Adele sprawled back in the carriage, her head lolling to one side and a bloodied hole at the front on her chest, the blood staining her fine clothing. He looked at her white face with her eyes still wide open, realising that the Marquise de Volanges was no longer of this world.

Sebastian watched from a distance at the commotion around Adele's carriage. He moved up to hear the comments of the people surrounding the carriage to learn that she was now dead.

He moved away to collect his horse tethered to a nearby tree, smiling triumphantly to himself, mounting quickly and wheeling his horse around, kicking the horse into a canter back onto the road to Paris.

Upon returning to the cheap boarding house, he strode quickly up the bare staircase to his room. He threw himself down on the hard bed placing the pistol on the bed stand nearby.

He lay back with his hands behind his head thinking of his life to come in his father's chateau which would be a very pale imitation of the glittering life he had lead at Versailles.

Pulling a flask of brandy from his hip pocket, he opened it and raising the flask to his lips he said 'Good riddance to you, Adele, you finished my life in Versailles and now yours is over too.'

❀

The Court was in uproar of Adele's death, not only as she was a distant member of the royal family, but also because it was well known that she was one of the King's favourite entertainers, although those close to Adele shed tears for show rather that those of genuine grief.

Marie-Therese took the news badly, needing much time alone in her rooms praying at her prie dieu for the soul of her aunt and that of the unknown perpetrator of the deed.

Her father, Edouard, seeing her at dinner a few weeks later was horrified to see how pale and how much thinner she had become. It distressed him how she picked at her food and showed little interest in the events around her. Edouard adored his daughter but due to his Ministerial duties, he had little time to spend with her.

After the meal finished, he took her aside and asked her what was troubling her. They talked quietly for some time looking out over the Palace orangery and Marie-Therese explained to him how deeply disillusioned she was with Court life.

Edouard held her to him, asking her what would make her life better for her as he couldn't bear to see her in this state any longer.

'Papa' she looked up at him with her large blue eyes, 'I have been thinking deeply over this. May I have your permission to leave Court and enter the sanctuary of a convent? I feel it would bring me peace of mind whereas all of this' she waved her arm dismissively at the Court where the after dinner gambling, dancing and licentious behaviour was evident and her voice petered out.

When Edouard didn't answer immediately, she hurried on 'I was thinking of the Royal Abbey of Fontevraud in the Loire where the royal children have been educated.'

As Edouard hugged his younger daughter, he realised he would have to grant her request although it would sadden him to be without her.

A few weeks later, on a bright morning, Edouard watched Marie-Therese climb into the carriage with wagons packed with her belongings lined up behind it for her journey to the Loire convent and her new life there. He looked into her face and noticed the brightness of her eyes now that she had a new purpose. 'I love you always, Papa, and thank you for making me so happy. You will be in my prayers daily'.

She saw Gabriel standing a way back from her father, and beckoned him forward. 'Dear Gabriel, I am sorry that we couldn't resolve matters but my heart has taken me in another direction.' He looked at her beautiful face and couldn't imagine her in a nun's clothing. He bowed low to avoid her seeing the anguish in his face.

Edouard and Gabriel watched, both heavy hearted, as the driver whipped up the horses and the carriage departed Versailles taking Marie-Therese to her new life.

Edouard felt great sadness as his favourite daughter left the Palace but part of him felt relieved that at least one daughter was safe now from the intrigues of the Court.

Sophia appeared not to notice that Marie-Therese had left the Court and tried to emulate Adele's success as an entertainer of the Court but failed miserably. She took to drinking more wine and brandy, starting earlier in the day, shouting at her servants and others drunkenly, gambling hard and losing money.

It wasn't long before she fell into disrepute having behaved badly whilst drunk in the presence of the King. Her latest beau was keen to take her bed, and some of her clothing had come adrift in the few moments of ardour before the King had arrived.

She tried to curtsy to him but nearly fell over before her friend grabbed her wrist and pulled her upright. She started to laugh until she saw the horrified looks on the faces of the King and the Marquise de Pompadour as they turned away in disgust especially as this wasn't the first time she had appeared drunk in public while the Court was in session.

Sophia had offended the Court by not following the strict rules of Court etiquette and was now shunned by most of the nobility. While it was not uncommon for the courtiers to drink or get drunk, no one was unwise enough to be inebriated right in front of the King.

Edouard gave her a stern talking to before dismissing her, telling her she would have to leave Court for the time being until her scandalous behaviour was forgotten. He also said that she should become more like her sister Marie-Therese, which infuriated Sophia. She knew her father favoured Marie-Therese over her but she was also angry that he thought she should become like her sister as she considered her to be so pious having gone into the convent.

Her anger and shame at having become a laughing matter at Court and being told by her father to leave the Court had dented her pride badly.

Disregarding her father's wishes, she continued drinking heavily. One night shortly afterwards, she was at her bedroom window looking at the full moon, a goblet of claret in hand. She looked back at her drunken lover snoring loudly in her bed annoyed at his poor performance earlier.

'Why do I feel so unfulfilled?' she asked herself

as tears slid down her face as she continued to pity herself and bemoan her state of affairs.

'What is the point of all this?' she mused, although in a rare moment of clarity, she recognised how privileged her life was here but pushed the thought away.

'I wish Aunt Adele, you were here, you would know what to do' she whispered to the moon.

The more she mused though, the angrier she got as she paced the room wildly as her lover continued to sleep unawares. She decided that everyone would be sorry at what they had done to her, as she threw her golden goblet across the room, the claret running down the wall.

She sobbed to herself, the tears pouring down her face. She knew that even her father preferred her sister and she desperately wished that Aunt Adele was here as she always solved all her problems.

'Why have you deserted me, Aunt Adele, why aren't you here to help me?' she sobbed again. She felt absolutely desolate. Then as her mood darkened further, in a fit of drunken despair, she opened her window wide, climbed out and threw herself from a great height to the ground below.

The next day when Edouard was informed of his beautiful elder daughter's death, he felt such sadness at her wasted life and wrote to Maria-

Therese to ask her to pray for her erstwhile sister.

'*My dearest daughter*' he wrote in his elegant script.

'*My heart is heavy with the news that your sister has been involved in an accident, having fallen from a window in the Palace and has perished as a result. I earnestly beg you to pray for her soul as her life here was somewhat dissolute despite my attempts at guidance.*

I think of you often, my sweet, and hope that you, at least, are happy in your new life.

I have tired of Court life and find the time has come for me to retire and I will go to my two sons and their families in Brittany and will write again to you from there.
Your ever loving father
Edouard.'

As he signed off his letter and handed to a servant to take to Marie-Therese at the Abbey, he felt old and disheartened with life.

He was tired too of his efforts of trying to please the King whilst also trying to guide him away from advice of the Marquise de Pompadour.

There had been much discussion amongst the Council Ministers as Machault d'Aurnouville and the Marquis d'Argenson, two of the King's very competent ministers, had been dismissed on the advice of the Marquise de Pompadour, who was now Louis confidante and advisor, They all had to tread carefully in case they offended the King's favourite leading to dismissal and Eduoard was very tired of it all.

Sighing deeply, Edouard, thought sorrowfully of Odette and how they had been cheated out of a lifetime together. Now both daughters were gone from Court, he would leave as soon as he could and go to his two sons and their growing families, praying for better family times.

After his mentor's departure, Gabriel stayed on at Versailles working himself hard to suppress the memories of what might have been, if circumstances hadn't taken such a dire turn. He missed Edouard and his companionship and advice; and Sebastian with the sharing of wine in the evenings discussing various subjects that they both found of interest.

He thought often of Marie-Therese and wondered how life might have turned out if only she had stayed at Versailles. He become more and more morose, refusing to join in the gambling and womanising which did nothing to endear him with his peers.

Instead, he concentrated on making a lot of money buying and selling property. He was also fluent in Latin, Italian and German, keeping himself busy in the daily workings of the Court successfully burying his emotions over Marie Therese.

One day while walking back to his rooms, he was startled as he thought he saw Marie-Therese walking through the Hall of Mirrors. His heart was racing as he quickly moved to catch up with her. To his disappointment it wasn't Marie-Therese but a young lady called Aloisia, who closely resembled Marie-Therese although somewhat younger.

She had the same small face and petite build but with green eyes instead of the deep blue of Marie-Therese's eyes.

He discovered she was German and in Versailles for a short time with her father who was there on Government business.

Gabriel quickly became enamored of her as she flirted with him. Aloisia's father saw a fine match in Gabriel encouraging his daughter in her pursuit of Gabriel.

Gabriel then made the horrendous mistake of marrying her. He quickly discovered that she was nothing like Marie-Therese in nature and her shrill voice and demands on his money caused him to feel wretched as he had neither the will or patience to remonstrate with his wife, giving in to her every demand.

Six months after they were married, they had travelled back to her homeland and her father's castle in the Rhine to see her family. One particular morning after she had irritated him beyond belief, he strode away from the breakfast room and made his way to the stables.

His head was pounding and he felt he had to get outside of the dark restrictive castle and the cloying family atmosphere. Aloisia's mother was very impressed with Gabriel and he had to make excuses to get away from her as she was constantly by his side asking his opinion on everything.

Gabriel picked out the best horse in the stables, a big, dark bay, to go for a ride. He smoothed his hand down the big gelding's neck murmuring greetings to him in German.

The groom thought it unwise to take the horse out as the air was heavy and the a thunderstorm was brewing, low rumbles of thunder being heard even as the stable boy lead the horse out to the yard. The groom didn't dare presume to mention his fears though to this wealthy man, who he had learned was one of the French aristocracy.

Gabriel leapt onto the back of the horse and charged out of the stables making for the green fields beyond. They hadn't gone far though, when a streak of lightening lit up the sky and the horse reared up before bolting across the fields.

Gabriel retained his seat initially before catching his head on a low hanging branch and falling to the ground. It was only when the horse had returned to the stables alone, now soaking wet in the pouring rain, that a party of men were dispatched to find Gabriel. They found him where he fell, his neck broken.

Sebastian, having returned to his father's château, mourned his old life at Versailles, making his new wife's life a misery. He felt lost without the intrigues of the Palace and his friend Gabriel and spent many days in a stupor from over indulgence of drinking to the despair of his family. It wasn't long before he died of an abscess of the liver.

The angels looked down and wept.

Chapter 7

Royal Abbey of Fontevraud
21 years later

Marie-Therese, was now known as Madeleine, after taking her vows into the church. She felt blessed to know the Abbess, Julie-Gillette de Pardaillan d'Antin, whom she had met when she first arrived here, distressed by events in Versailles. Julie-Gillette helped her find peace and had become her mentor and friend.

Time passed and her life fell into a serene pattern following the devotions of her faith, gardening and helping the poor.

It was the twenty first year of her living at the convent and a particularly cold winter came upon them. Marie-Therese never understood how the poor folk in the surrounding countryside managed to survive and spent many hours at the Abbey gates ministering to the beggars gathered there, the left over food from the convent.

The sky was a pewter grey and the frost was hard on the ground.

Passing one of the windows, the Abbess saw Marie-Therese standing at the gates and frowned, as it had been some hours that Marie-

Therese had been out there, dealing with the never ending stream of beggars. She sent a young nun out immediately to bring Marie-Therese back to the warmth of the Abbey.

She ushered Marie-Therese into her study and sat her by the fire. Her spare frame was shivering and her lips looked blue with cold. The Abbess knew it was useless to admonish her about staying out in the cold for so long, instead she ordered a hot posset of milk and wine to warm her up.

Marie-Therese looked up into her friend's kind face and was very grateful that she took the trouble to look after her, as she was so easily absorbed by her work. She gratefully drank the posset and stayed by the fire while the Abbess continued working at her desk until the evening shadows began to fall and the bell rang for Vespers.

That night Marie-Therese felt unwell and now lay on her narrow hard bed and looked around the cell that had been her home in for so long. The small brazier in her room with the burning coals cast shadows around the room and gave out a little heat. She started to shiver and then felt so hot and then chilled again until she could no longer tell the difference.

She became delirious and her cries brought another nun to her cell who having seen Marie-Therese condition, immediately alerted the Abbess.

Maria-Therese continued mumbling, occasionally lashing out an arm as though trying to ward someone off.

The Abbess stayed with her throughout the night, sitting on a small stool by the bed, trying out different herbal concoctions, bathing her head and body with a cloth to try and take the heat out of Marie-Therese's body but to no avail.

Just before sunrise, as the sky began to lighten, Marie-Therese briefly opened her eyes, looking at the crucifix on the wall above her prie dieu. She smiled briefly at her friend before her eyes closed again.

As she lay on the bed, she felt a great sense of peace as she became aware of a soft, rose coloured portal. Feeling herself move forward towards it by a gentle pulling sensation, she then saw a brilliant light coming towards her. Marie-Therese realised that she was now able to see vast distances with beautiful scenery with a feeling of being surrounded in a warm, welcoming love.

The candlelight in the cell flickered suddenly and then went out although there was no draught and the Abbess knew then that Marie-Therese was no longer with her.

The Abbess crossed herself and bit her lip as her friend's spirit passed, knowing that she must not show emotion in front of the postulate nun who was also present. The Abbey rules were that having friends here was not allowed; they were only here to love and serve God.

She checked Marie-Therese's life signs to confirm what she already knew.

The Abbess, ever a practical woman, then moved quickly starting the events of storing the body in the ice house where it would have to be kept for a while as the ground was too frozen for a grave to be dug just yet.

Part 2

Chapter 8

Return to the spiritual realm

Marie-Therese awoke and thought she was still in her cell but felt a deep sense that things were subtly different. She thought she remembered a dream of rising rapidly through a stream of colours before landing on firm ground.

As she looked through the window of her room, she saw the most beautiful tranquil gardens pulsating with colours unlike anything she had seen before. She drew a quick breath as she took it all in.

Then she became aware of a serene energy manifesting beside her and as she looked up she saw the kindest and wisest face she had ever seen.

Marie-Therese knew she had sensed the energy from this person many times in her life but had never acknowledged it before. Instinctively, she understood that this light being was her guide who had been looking out for her the entire time she was on the earth plane and who was now sending her energy to help her.

They moved effortlessly from her cell into another room in a part of a beautiful marble building which held a very peaceful atmosphere almost as though the building itself was sending her vibrations of complete love.

She understood that she could now boost her soul energy in this crystal room where prisms of cleansing light were reflected across the room in beautiful colours giving her clarity to her thoughts.

Once she felt refreshed, she returned to her guide who was waiting nearby. Wordlessly, she exchanged thoughts with her guide who was asking her how she felt about the life she had just left. Marie-Therese was astonished to realise that she had no regrets about leaving the convent and was supremely happy to be where she was now.

The atmosphere of absolute and complete love was unlike anything she had felt on Earth, even in the Abbey and she found it so wonderful to be cocooned in love like this. Her guide sat with her while she became more aware of her change in circumstances and adjusted to them. Her guide then indicated that it was now time for her to meet her Council of Elders with whom she had previously discussed her earthly life in France before leaving the spiritual realm.

She and her guide moved into a domed room where the diffused lights glowed everywhere. In front of them was a long table with five light beings sitting there.

The Elders appeared to have auras in colours of purple, pure white and gold which indicated the high levels of their spiritual growth. Her guide stood behind her slightly to the left, as another wordless conversation took place between Marie-Therese and them.

Maria-Therese felt no sense of judgment but a compassionate and harmonious atmosphere where a loving discussion was held about what had happened in her life and the decisions she had made as a consequence.

Questions were asked gently about why she made certain decisions in major episodes of her life and whether she had any regrets. Had her body served her well? What was the intent in her life? Was she submerged by events or was she able to rise above her difficulties?

One of the Elders asked her whether leaving Versailles to spend the rest of her life in the convent was satisfactory for her.

She responded that she felt she had made the right decision becoming a nun to further her spiritual quest and offer sustenance to the poor and needy who came to the convent.

In return she received such a sense of complete love from the Elders, unlike anything she had ever experienced before. The love was almost overwhelming in its purity and the joy it gave her.

The lights in the room changed again to a very soft blue and Marie-Therese knew it was the moment to leave the meeting of the Elders. She moved away from the table, thanking them for their patience and love.

Her guide then took her to another part of the crystal building where she found herself in a room with others where the energy and atmosphere was one of celebration. She had returned to her soul group with whom she worked with before, both here and on the Earth to learn and grow spiritually.

She moved through one soul group closely connected to her own, recognising some of them from France: an elderly nun who had taught her the ways of the convent when she had first arrived and two others whom she had helped: a man and wife who begged outside the convent.

She smiled at them, clasping their hands briefly before moving into her own soul group where she saw her parents, Odette and Eduoard who came forward and hugged her. She saw Mathilde, her mother's close friend standing to one side who greeted her with a huge smile.

Her parents looked at her with pride. They told her that she had done so well helping others and didn't allow the emotional pain from the events in Versailles to blight her life.

Her guide now returned to her with the residue

of her soul energy which all souls leave in the spiritual realm while working on Earth. She now absorbed that portion of her soul energy back into her light body giving her a feeling of strength, security and identity; a deep pink light tinged with gold emanating from her now.

She turned and saw Gabriel, Sebastian, Adele and Sophia standing nearby. They looked so happy, radiant and younger than she remembered, free of earthly constraints and petty actions.

Gabriel came forward first, his arms open to her. She gladly went to him now understanding the events of Versailles and the learning curve that those events had created for them both. She saw now that they had to learn the lesson of emotional balance and personal responsibility whilst being apart.

She looked at Adele and Sebastian seeing their close connection but that their lives and arrogant attitudes in Versailles gave others the opportunity to react in either a positive or negative way to what had transpired.

Marie-Therese also realised that they had decided to live a tumultuous life in order to understand and learn more of the turbulent emotions which they had created with their actions.

They came forward with joy at seeing her again and the celebratory reception continued with deep love and camaraderie, hugs, laughter and humour as they all celebrated her return to their soul group.

Marie-Therese looked at Sophia whose aura of white with tinges of pink had the colours of a younger soul.

She was still learning from others around her, which is why she was in this more advanced soul group to grow and understand more of her potential.

When Sophia had her meeting with the Elders, no judgment had been made on her suicide in Versailles however, the Elders had given her suggestions of how to move past the thinking that had precipitated her suicide.

Sophia's first communication to Marie-Therese was asking her whether she wanted to return to Earth immediately as she, Sophia, couldn't wait to get back to the sensory pleasures and delights on Earth.

Maria-Therese saw Sophia's guide standing nearby and was aware of the guide's loving thoughts that Sophia would learn more on her next foray onto the physical plane.

Marie-Therese now knew that no soul was looked down upon but received kindness, tolerance, patience and absolute love from the guides.

A guiding spiritual principle is that wrongdoing, intentional or otherwise can be redressed in another lifetime.

After Marie-Therese had orientated herself back in her spiritual home she became aware that there were opportunities to attend lectures and classes and spiritual work to perform as well as periods of relaxation and fun. There was never any judgment, just lots of love and laughter.

She loved to sit in the beautiful gardens filled with heavily scented flowers which glowed in colours unlike anything she had seen on Earth. Beyond the gardens were lakes and beyond them, awe inspiring scenery of countryside and purple coloured mountains.

Marie-Therese loved to gaze at the scenery feeling a deep sense of peace and serenity. She discovered quickly that whatever scenery she wanted to experience, she only had to think of it and connect mentally with the energy vibration of that place and she was immediately transported there. She shook her head in astonishment the first time it had happened.

She found that there were many activities she enjoyed and would also meet with others in a sparkling white domed building with small rooms attached to large corridors which seemed to stretch away into infinity.

In one activity, Marie-Therese worked in a classroom setting with a teacher called Cecilia, who emanated the colour pink tinged with green in her aura, her face shining with enthusiasm for her pupils.

Whilst in this group, Marie-Therese would dwell in pure thought to come up with ideas that would be of benefit to everyone.

There were also times when Maria-Therese returned to the Earth level as an invisible being to lend loving energy to others struggling with their lives.

However, the favourite part of Maria-Therese work was to join with others making harmonious waves of pure sound to transmit to the leaders on Earth. These waves vibrationally smoothed out the mental aggravation to calm the leaders' minds, helping them make the right decisions for those who elected them to high office. Great swathes of blue light were transmitted to Earth during this activity.

After working they rested and socialised, talking, learning from one another. Beautiful lights played through the area together with harmonious music.

Marie-Therese worked with the others and used this time to absorb information from each others life experiences. They looked as the way they handled feelings and emotions while on earth, with humour, tolerance, forgiveness and love knowing that the negative traits connected to their egos which brought them sadness and heartache when they were on Earth, now no longer existed.

Whilst enjoying all her activities, Marie-Therese felt, after a long while, the pull to return to Earth in order to experience more of the challenges presented there which would help her grow more quickly at her soul level.

She realised that Gabriel, Sebastian, Adele and Sophie were ready to return to an earthly life again too, so now it was time for all of them to work out new life plans.

There was an intense desire to prove themselves worthy of the trust placed in them together with the feeling of humility at having been given the opportunity to incarnate in physical form again. They all knew now that making mistakes in this process were expected, however the learning they absorbed whilst in the physical form would help the greater good of all, which was a great motivator to return to Earth.

Now they were together in a beautiful yellow crystal building where their life reviews were taking place. The air shimmered with gold light. They sat together in a circle where, with their guides, they reviewed their time in France and saw how things could have turned out differently.

The scene was then set to plan for their new lives and they reviewed and picked their new body types and tried out various scenarios to see what may happen and what choices they may make.

They were all made aware that whilst they were formulating their new life plans they also had the free will to alter their plans if they so desired.

Although they all understood that returning to Earth was with a focus on what still needed to be learned for their soul's growth.

In their reviews the Elders had asked each of them the question 'What would you like to achieve in the next lifetime?'

Difficulties they had experienced in their last lives were discussed and complaints were dealt with lovingly, with counselling and suggestions.

Sophia complained of her lack of success and admiration from others in Versailles and was gently told 'Go back and see what you can do this time.'

They were guided carefully through their choices as Earth was considered the most challenging of planes to work within. Exit points from their lifetime was also offered, giving them choices of when they may wish to return home to the spiritual level.

They understood that their destiny on Earth was the sum of choices made over many incarnations and this was the opportunity to learn further but could use their free will as well to change their pathways at any time if they wanted.

They were advised to consciously use any challenges to foster spiritual growth; to understand that the people in their lives, including parents and children are there at their request, motivated by their love, to play out certain roles that they have scripted here before leaving.

If difficult situations occurred, it was suggested that they try to replace anger, guilt and blame with forgiveness and acceptance if they could.

If one of them wanted to experience rejection, abandonment, or some other difficult emotion in the human form, another soul may agree to take on the role of a nemesis to invoke this type of experience. So they would know that in the eyes of an enemy, a friendly soul may be looking lovingly back helping their growth, although they may not be aware of it at the time.

It was all a soul-expanding process which would deepen greatly with appreciation and gratitude for life.

At the start of the process to return to Earth, Marie-Therese found it fascinating to be present in her mother's womb, at times watching the new body's foetus growing. It was transparent and she could see the organs developing with it's little heart beating. She went in and out of the foetus for some time to get used to the feeling of being back in a restrictive physical body.

She pushed her soul energy in to the limbs and head knowing that she would eventually join the foetus permanently and was feeling excited to be starting another cycle of learning.

Adele, as an older soul, had picked a challenging experience in her Versailles life time. She had experienced a life of self indulgence and adulation although lack of trust from others due to her court intrigues had made it a lonely life. She knew that Sebastian would be with her this time to help her as she planned to support Sophia who seemed unwilling to change her desires for another lifetime of indulgence on Earth.

Gabriel knew that this time, he and Marie-Therese would be together at some point in their Earthly sojourn and he had a determination that they would stay together this time around.

Marie-Therese acknowledged that she would carry no memories of her life and decisions made in the spiritual world or her past lives as this would be too much for her earthly mind to understand. The challenge was to rise above the difficulties.

She also knew that she could use free will to change her life plan if she so wished.

She recognised that it was important to have gratitude for her new life and to know that everyone who connects with their spirituality has assistance and support in life for whatever lay ahead. However those who don't connect may manifest addictions and perhaps depression or anger, in order to draw attention to their need to reconnect with their spirituality.

She hoped too, that at some level she would remember that all souls are equal in the spiritual realm despite any negative traits they may show on Earth and that her mission was to help others on the pathway wherever possible.

This was something Marie-Therese desperately wanted to remember as she felt this would have been of great assistance to her living through her time in Versailles.

The day arrived of her birth and she felt a tremendous urge to be born to start another cycle. She was a small baby and the midwife exclaimed as she placed her in her mother's arms 'She is beautiful, just like a little doll.'

Part 3

Brighton and Hove
Present day

These are the names of those reincarnated from Versailles to Brighton.

Marie-Therese /Amber
Sebastian /Jonathan
Adele / Nancy
Sophia / Harriet, now the sister of Adele/Nancy
Gabriel / Alexander who lives next door to Jonathan and Nancy
Odette / Clara
Edouard / Benjamin
Mathilde / Matilda

Chapter 9

The music was playing very loudly. There were two men sitting in the living room of the Bedford Towers apartment high above the Holiday Inn on Kings Road in Brighton.

Jonathan leaned back on the black leather sofa, closing his eyes as he inhaled from the joint that he and his next door neighbour, Alexander, were sharing.

He was enjoying a well earned break from running his night club, called Phoenix, in Mayfair. He was tall and lanky with floppy blond shoulder length hair and had been mistaken for the actor, Bill Nighy several times. His younger companion, Alexander, was of a stockier build with dark hair, his best feature being his very blue eyes.

Harriet walked furtively into Cavendish Place from Kings Road and up the steps to the main entrance to Bedford Towers. She pressed the intercom button repeatedly as she couldn't find her house keys but could get no response from her sister Nancy or her brother in law Jonathan, who owned the apartment.

She swore to herself as she felt vulnerable standing in Cavendish Place, just off Brighton seafront. She removed the large sunglasses she was wearing to help conceal her face, as she dug into her voluminous designer handbag for her mobile.

Jonathan's mobile buzzed and vibrated on the coffee table in front of him and raising his eyebrows to Alexander, he took his sister in law's call. Abusive language greeted him, as Harriet raged at him that she couldn't get in to the entrance foyer.

He ambled across the room and turned the music down before going to the intercom to allow his sister in law in.

At that moment, Nancy, flew in from the kitchen with her knife in her hand. 'Why did you turn down Pavarotti? You know that Nessun Dorma is my favourite piece of music' she said, her brown eyes wide and annoyance on her tanned face.

Jonathan subconsciously rubbed his shoulder where he had a birthmark displayed in the shape of a ragged tear. 'Hey Nanc' he drawled, 'your sis is yelling that she can't get in because we couldn't hear the intercom with the music playing.'

Nancy looked back at him, rolling her eyes dismissively, running her hand absently over pearl choker at her throat before returning to the kitchen to finish the food for the dinner party she was giving.

Alexander looked at Jonathan 'Wow, she looked a bit fierce, didn't she?'

'No worries, she doesn't mean it, just her way of expressing herself sometimes.'

Harriet then burst into the room, a sulky expression on her face. She threw down her coat and handbag on the empty sofa opposite Jonathan and Alexander before collapsing into a large armchair, facing the view of the sun setting over the horizon. The beauty of the sunset missed her completely as she was totally self absorbed as usual.

'Pass me that joint' she commanded Jonathan who duly did as he was asked. Harriet threw back her head as she exhaled, swinging her long elegant legs over the arm of the chair.

Alexander looked on, seeing her long dark hair and pretty face with a tiny mole on her cheek but feeling distaste at her behaviour. He had only meet her a couple of times, but she struck him as a selfish individual and so different in nature to her sister Nancy.

Nancy returned to the sitting room with the hors d'oeuvres saying 'Time to eat'. Harriet reluctantly put out the joint and then joined the others at the elaborate dining table.

Alexander asked 'What fantastic food have we today, Nancy?' as he sat down taking his napkin from the table. Nancy grinned at him as

Jonathan laughed at Alexander 'You only say that so you get extra food, you greedy bugger.'

'Stop it' Nancy admonished her husband before turning back to Alexander saying 'I decided to practice my Cordon Bleu skills from my recent cooking course in London.

'It is a completely French menu' Nancy said ticking off the courses on her fingers, 'my home made liver paté, followed by cassoulet with duck, pork and beans. I bought some lovely French cheeses from the market and then made floating islands for dessert.'

'The floating islands sound interesting. What are they then?' Alexander queried, tilting his head slightly.

'They are meringues floating on creme anglaise,' Nancy responded with pride.

Jonathan said 'They are worth waiting for' as he turned back from the audio system where he was putting on some soft background music as the dinner commenced.

Nancy raised her glass and said 'I have just realised that today would have been Clara's ninety third birthday, if she had lived.'

Jonathan raised his glass too saying to Alexander 'Clara was Nancy and Harriet's grandmother' pointing to a photograph on the French cabinet near the dining table.

'That's Clara with her husband Benjamin.' Nancy continued.

Alexander looked up at the photograph and saw that Nancy took after her grandmother where Harriet's looks came from another part of the family. Alexander held up his glass too and together they toasted Clara.

Nancy continued the story, explaining to Alexander 'Our parents died in a car crash in France when we were quite young so our grandparents looked after us.'

She carried on 'They left us some money a few years ago and I invested in this apartment although someone else managed to spend all of her inheritance' her eyes moving over to Harriet who wasn't taking the slightest interest in the conversation.

We love this place, don't we Jonathan?' she said putting her hand over Jonathan's long fingers.

'Yes, we do' he responded 'we love our house in London too but, of course, we don't have the sea views like here and it is great to get away for a while from running my nightclub.'

There was a pause in the conversation before Alex said 'I know I keep saying it, but you are a brilliant chef, Nancy' wiping his mouth with a napkin as he finished the paté, sweeping breadcrumbs to one side that he had littered on the table.

Nancy smiled at him as she poured him another glass of the rich red Chateauneuf du Pape before serving the cassoulet.

The dinner table discussions then turned to Alexander's new business project. He was opening a shop in Brighton's North Laines offering regression hypnotherapy, acupuncture and tarot readings.

Jonathan grinned wryly saying 'Maybe you could get a tarot reading done for Harriet to get her out of her mess.'

Harriet didn't even look up from her mobile 'Fat chance, load of rubbish' was her retort which confirmed to Alexander just what a thoughtless individual she was, not concerned with how others felt, and obviously believed she was in charge of her own fate.

Nancy winced at Harriet's rudeness but changed the subject by asking Jonathan 'Will you get the Beaumes de Venise to go with the dessert, Jonathan?'

Nancy asked Alexander whether he had tried this dessert wine before continuing 'I really love this dessert wine from the Rhone Valley however, in the French tradition, we will be having the cheeseboard first'.

They all knew that Nancy was really into her French cuisine and they really appreciated it.

Harriet having just finished her large glass of red wine returned to looking at her mobile phone. 'Will you put that damn thing away' her sister demanded. 'It is just so rude when other people are here'.

Harriet looked back at her. 'You know I need to keep up with my Twitter account after what has happened, you idiot' she responded offensively.

'Well, if you hadn't been stupid in the first place, nothing would have happened would it?' Nancy said over her shoulder as she returned to the kitchen to collect the cheeses.

'Oh Nancy, just cool it will you?' Jonathan said, 'We have a guest here.'

He could hear Nancy slamming things around in the kitchen but determinedly kept up his conversation with Alexander, ignoring Harriet's muttered responses to what she was seeing on her mobile.

Chapter 10

Harriet had not needed to flaunt her association with Jonathan to get past the queue waiting outside his nightclub in London.

The bouncers at the front door knew her and would have let her in anyway as she was exactly the type of clientele that the nightclub required.

They watched admiringly as she flounced up to the entrance, her slim statuesque figure in clothing that emphasised her breasts and her tight black leather skirt showing off her long legs. She wore no coat despite the cold weather.

Once inside, she could hear the pounding beat of the music however she didn't go towards the dance floor, instead she immediately climbed the sweeping staircase and made her way into the voile curtained area where red leather sofas were spread around the room.

Her practiced eye took in the various people, lounging on the sofas checking out if there were any famous people present yet.

She took a seat on the end of an empty sofa before ordering her favourite cocktail, an old classic called a Negroni, from a passing waitress. The waitress, Bela, stood for a moment waiting to see if there was a thank you coming from Harriet but Harriet just waved her away.

After placing Harriet's drink order at the bar, Bela and her colleague, Anne, were discussing Harriet's condescending manners. Along with the other waitresses, they were both young and pretty, picked for their looks.

'Just who does she think she is?' Bela muttered.

'Stuck up prig if you ask me', responded her friend.

'She never leaves a tip either' snorted Anne.

'Oh, just look who has turned up'. Bela turned to see a man looking into the room through a gap in the curtains.

The man Harriet was waiting to meet arrived shortly after her cocktail had been set down in front of her. She saw him looking into the room but deliberately ignored him, sweeping her long dark hair over one shoulder.

He was tall with a smooth tanned countenance, grey swept back hair and an obvious air of confidence as he walked across the room before joining her on the sofa. He commanded a passing waiter to bring a bottle of Verve Clicquot champagne immediately.

Harriet was secretly pleased that she had been able to pick up this man, a well known Member of Parliament and had been his mistress for the last few months.

She had had enough of trying to pay her own way in the world and decided that the life of a mistress to a well heeled man would work wonders for her bank balance, and he was currently proving to be ideal.

Harriet smiled at him sweetly as they sipped champagne listening to the music vibrating upwards from the dance floor below. 'Henry, darling, what lovely champagne,' she said in her husky voice which he had said turned him on.

He moved closer and as he put his arm up on the back of the leather button backed sofa behind her, she could smell the aroma of his distinctive aftershave.

'And what have you in store for me tonight?' he whispered in her ear. She smiled knowingly at him, giving him a light laugh, 'You will have to wait and see', as she ran her fingers down his beautifully tailored shirt.

Another bottle of champagne quickly followed and Harriet looked adoringly into his eyes as they talked.

Bela, laughing, got out her mobile phone and said to Anne 'I'm going to video this, he's a married man.' 'No' Anne said quickly 'You know the boss' policy on privacy, that is why the rich and famous come here, because they know they won't be spied upon.'

'I don't care', was Bela's response, 'They won't know who took it, they are bombed after what they have been snorting up their noses.' She carefully manoeuvered herself behind the gap between the curtains and aimed her phone at the couple now sprawled out on the sofa.

Anne took a breath in, horrified that Bela was disregarding the club's privacy policy with the risk of dismissal if found out.

Bela triumphantly switched off the video and said 'I know what else I am going to do too' she said grimly to Anne. 'I am going to call up Jack, my photographer friend and get him to take photos of them when they leave. We can sell the photos to the newspapers and I can make some money to pay my student loan.'

Anne shook her head in amazement, waving her hand at Bela in a dismissive gesture and walked away, not willing to be party to what Bela was doing.

Bela stepped to one side of the room and made her call to Jack who readily agreed to split the money from selling the photos to the newspapers.

At midnight, Henry thought he had done enough to get Harriet to go back to his flat which he used during the week while at Westminster.

They left, as usual, by the back door rather than face the crowd at the front of the club still waiting to get in.

Bela nearly missed their departure but quickly phoned Jack just giving him enough time to get in position outside the back door of the club from the coffee shop where he had been waiting for Bela's call.

Jack discreetly took photographs of Harriet and Henry as they stumbled out of the club, busy kissing and exploring each other's bodies before practically falling into the waiting cab. Jack quickly hopped on his scooter and followed them to Henry's flat in Knightsbridge, taking more photos as they entered the smart apartment building.

The following weekend, the Sunday newspapers were full of the photographs of the pair leaving the club and entering Henry's flat with the video also on YouTube showing them sprawled on the sofa, being amorous with each other in the nightclub.

They were pilloried in the press. The story of the married MP with four children, the Minister who recently publicly berated an Opposition MP for immoral conduct, cavorting in a nightclub and taking a young woman back to his flat, drew a backlash from the more conservative newspapers, whereas the tabloids revelled in the disaster of his own making.

So Harriet was now hiding out with her sister and brother in law in Brighton waiting for the furore to die down.

Chapter 11

Alex met Amber at a psychic show in Brighton two weeks before where he was advertising his new business of holistic practices.

Amber had liked him from the moment she saw him and readily sat down to hear what his business could offer.

She had admitted to him that she had found most of the stalls unexciting and felt the show was just for the practitioners to make money out of the crowd.

She learned that he owned several properties in Brighton and rented them out, as well as doing translation work for a company in London. He was interested in the paranormal and had decided to open a small business with experienced therapists to learn more about his new hobby.

They went for a drink after the show closed at the Hixon Green bar on Church Road and when they parted Alex suggested they might like to meet up again.

Amber said 'I have to go on a business trip but will be back in a couple of weeks, would that work for you?'

Feeling reckless, Alex offered Amber Sunday lunch on her return.

They were at the dining table in Alex's flat and Amber asked 'What made you decide to go into the holistic business, then?' Before he could answer, she continued 'I love this chicken and tarragon dish by the way, where did you buy it?'

'I bought it, oh' he paused 'that's me busted then' laughing out loud.

'How did you know that I didn't cook it myself?' Amber grinned 'Your kitchen and your utensils all look new and hardly used.'

'There's no fooling you then, is there?' he grinned back.

Amber leaned back in her chair and picked up her wineglass as Alex continued to speak.

'So, to answer your question on why I have gone into the holistic business. When I was in London working for the translation agency about eighteen months ago, a girl there was very much into her spirituality and talked of auras, chakras, reincarnation, karma and other ideas which got me to thinking along those lines.

I have done quite a lot of research and decided to open a business although I have experienced therapists to do the work as I am still learning about different philosophies.'

'How do you know whether your workers have integrity? I felt at the psychic show that a lot of the practitioners were only in it for the money.'

'Yes, you did say that at the time' he responded. 'Well, I would like to think that I am a reasonable judge of character and I obviously ask my therapists for their work experience.

I also ask my clients to fill in a feedback form at the end of the session about what they thought of the service and the therapist. I know it isn't a foolproof system however, I talk to my practitioners a lot and try to get a feel for their philosophy and whether they are the right fit for what I want to provide.'

Amber nodded 'I agree, a lot of what people say can give a clear indication of how they are thinking. For example, I heard someone say recently that he loved to point out other peoples mistakes, which I thought was sad. It made me wonder why that was necessary and why he had to make himself feel better by belittling others.'

Alex responded Yes, let me think' he paused, 'that was very similar to what Julia, my colleague in London, said. 'Yes,' he sat thinking for a moment and then continued, 'Julia maintained that if you have your own spiritual philosophy and take emotional responsibility for yourself, it makes you a more grounded person who doesn't judge others. And as a result you don't need other people to validate you.'

Amber said thoughtfully 'I like those ideas as I would like to think that we can help each through life rather than be unkind'.

Their discussion continued through the meal and afterwards, they were lying together on the sofa finishing a bottle of Macon Village wine as the rain lashed at the windows.

Amber commented 'I don't think I have ever seen you wear socks, do you have a phobia about them?' she queried, looking up into his face.

'No, no I don't think so' Alex replied grinning at her 'I just prefer bare feet, I think I was born to live in the sun always'.

'Me too' she replied.

Alex replied thoughtfully, 'I could get Claire, my regression hypnotherapist, to regress me and I could find out where I lived in past lives. I have been thinking about giving it a go.'

'How does that work then?' Amber queried.

'Well is starts off like a regular hypnotherapy session to relax your body and mind and then Claire talks you through a guided meditation which will hopefully take you back to a previous lifetime. She then asks you questions about that lifetime and what you are seeing. For example, it can help to find out what lessons and experiences you had in that past life and what relevance it has on your present lifetime. That is of course, if you believe in reincarnation. Apparently, it can also help sort out things like phobias and nightmares' he concluded.

'That would be brilliant for me, I would think, as from childhood I have had visions of huge waves crashing down on me and we didn't even live near the sea when I was a child. I have no idea where that came from' responded Amber.

'Well, that would certainly be worth investigating. Let's see what we can arrange, it might be very interesting to see what we get and I wonder if maybe we have met before in another lifetime' he said giving her a hug.

A feeling jolted through Amber which only confirmed to her that there seemed to be a connection between them. She drank some more wine quickly to cover her confusion.

The following week, Amber was standing in Alex's shop in the North Laines feeling a little anxious about having a regression done. The shop was freshly painted in white with a small reception area with the therapy rooms behind it.

The young receptionist smiled at Amber as she confirmed her booking and as she did so, Alex came out from one of the rooms, a large smile appearing on his face when he saw Amber.

He looked at her slight figure, her sparkling blue eyes and her long blonde bob haircut feeling very pleased that she here having decided to try out the therapy.

He took her hand and drew her down to the two white leather seats in the waiting area.

'Tell me about your regression which you had the other day' she said, smiling back at him.

'Well, it was very interesting' he said 'I didn't get any past life in the sun,' looking down at his bare feet 'but a life in the Court of Versailles! I was amazed', he continued 'I felt very much at home there and worked hard for King Louis in the 1700s with building projects I think. I could see architect's plans although it wasn't that clear. I knew it was Versailles because I saw the Palace looking like the picture I have here on the wall in my office.

Claire, the hypnotherapist, asked me questions and I saw a lot of other detail. It seems I have something to learn from that life time that is relevant to this one. I think you may have been there too, although I couldn't be sure it was you.'

He laughed 'Although you have been on my mind a lot so maybe I was just imagining it'.

They agreed it would be very interesting to see what her regression would bring her and whether she would possibly see him.

Amber felt this was an excellent way to discover more about herself and her life and now she couldn't wait to start her regression session. She had this strange feeling that she was missing some people in her life and wondered if she could find an answer through this hypnotherapy.

Claire, a tall girl with brown hair and a New Zealand accent came out and collected Amber from the reception area, taking her through to the therapy room. Alex flashed her a reassuring smile as she went.

The room was dimly light with soft music playing quietly. Amber moved onto the couch in the centre of the room making herself comfortable before Claire covered her with a blanket.

'Your body temperature can drop while lying still so I recommend covering you up while we have this session. Have you ever had a regression before?'

'No, I haven't' replied Amber.

'Well there is nothing to be concerned about, but if you feel uneasy about anything, you will be able to tell me.'

Having established that Amber was good at visualisation, Claire then proceeded to talk quietly, taking Amber through some relaxation exercises, asking her to imagine her favourite place so if she felt any concerns, she could imagine herself in this safe place.

After which she asked Amber to visualise a cloud, and her climbing onto it and travelling through time and space. When the cloud drifted to the ground and stopped, Amber was asked to move away from the cloud and to look down at her feet, initially to see what shoes she had on, as this was one of the easiest ways to connect to a past lifetime.

As the session went on, Amber was able to see herself living a life as a nun in France a few centuries ago. She knew she was a wealthy woman who had retired to the convent to escape the life she had been living.

She didn't get a lot more detail, however Claire reassured her that further sessions may bring more information.

Amber was disappointed that she didn't get anything to do with Versailles like Alex. Her life as a French nun, however helped her understand that her focus in that life was on spiritual matters which was perhaps why she felt the same way now.

She thought she would have more regressions which she hoped would help her become more aware of what she was supposed to be doing in this lifetime and perhaps see if she did have a past connection with Alex.

The following weekend, Alex took Amber for a trip up the 1360 tower on the seafront, a short walk from his flat. The British Airways staff who worked the 1360 experience, treated it like they were going on an actual flight.

They queued up, having bought their tickets from the replica Victorian booth and walked through the glass door onto the balcony. After the pod had descended and the occupants exited, they were able to walk into the clear glass pod that would move up the central core slowly and stop at the top for them to see the coastline view.

Amber had gasped in astonishment as the pod moved effortlessly upwards, allowing amazing views to be seen. She didn't realise the pod was moving until the scenery started to change, as it was so quiet.

Alex asked if she was coping with the height as the pod stopped at the top so the passengers could walk around and look at the different aspects of the town and seascape.

'I just love it' Amber responded 'just look, we can see where you live and even where I am in York Avenue. It is wonderful.'

Alex looked at her awed expression and squeezed her hand. He was not going to let on that he was finding it unsettling to be so high, looking out through the floor to ceiling glass, and he held on tight to the railing support with his other hand.

Once the pod had descended, they stepped out and exited through the gift shop, Alex told Amber that they had been invited to Jonathan and Nancy's for sun downer drinks.

Amber smiled in delight at the thought of meeting Alex's neighbours as she had heard such good things about them. She knew that Alex enjoyed their company a great deal.

They waited at the roadside for a break in the traffic, crossing diagonally for the short walk from the i360 complex to Cavendish Place and the entrance to the flats.

Alex told her that the owners living in the flats above the Holiday Inn, had access to all the gym facilities and swimming pool in the hotel. 'Perhaps you would like to come for a swim sometime?' he asked. Amber agreed willingly.

They entered the foyer and took the lift up to the top floor to Jonathan and Nancy's apartment.

As soon as they arrived, Amber was greeted with kisses on both cheeks by Nancy and Jonathan.

Nancy smiled at Amber, 'Please come through' and together they went into the large sunlit living area where Jonathan moved over to the bar to prepare their drinks.

'What did you think of the I360?' Nancy enquired. Amber turned to her smiling 'It was amazing, I could see where I live and right up the coast to the Isle of Wight. It was fantastic because I could see so far but then you have wonderful views from up here too, don't you?'

Nancy looked at her and smiled. 'Yes, we are very fortunate but that was a major reason for buying here. It isn't a pretty sight with the tall tower' she continued 'but I guess if people want the views it is worth it for them to go up into the pod.'

She asked Amber 'Would you like a cocktail? Jonathan makes a mean one'.

She and Jonathan smiled at her comment and Alex said 'Make mine a White Russian please. Sorry,' he continued looking at Nancy's face, 'That was a bit rude of me, jumping in like that.'

Nancy gave him a smile in return.

Jonathan looked at Amber's uncertain face. She said 'I don't really drink cocktails, so I don't know much about them except that I get drunk quite quickly when I have them.'

Nancy smiled at her 'How about a Kir Royale and sip it slowly then?'

'Oh yes, I like that, it has a liqueur added to the champagne doesn't it?' queried Amber. Nancy said 'Yes that's right, champagne and crème de cassis, which is a blackcurrant liqueur.'

'Oh yes please, that sounds wonderful, thank you.'

Jonathan looked at Nancy 'And how about you, sweetie?'

'Martini please, darling' came the reply. 'What are you having?'

Jonathan replied 'I think I will have a Manhattan'.

Jonathan busied himself at the bar and when the cocktails were completed, they walked out on to the balcony. Nancy had put out olives, nuts and crisps on the table and Amber gratefully took some, so the champagne didn't go straight to her head. She didn't want to appear even a little drunk in front of people she didn't know well.

The air was warm for the time of year with the sun casting a red path across the sea as it began to set.

Amber took an immediate liking to Jonathan with his laid back manner and thought Nancy was a delight, making her feel very welcomed. She was thrilled that at last her social life was on the up. She marvelled that at last she had found some people with whom she felt so familiar with immediately and was enjoying their hospitality so much.

They talked animatedly for some time and Jonathan was generous with topping up their glasses. Nancy had explained to Amber how they came to have this apartment but also had a house in Eaton Square in London.

'Have you always lived in Brighton. Amber?'

Amber looked at her 'No, I decided to move to Brighton from Hurstpierpoint after my mother died last year and I felt I needed a change of scenery. She left me some money so I have an apartment in a building called Aylesbury on York Avenue near here.'

As Amber's eyes welled up at the memory of her mother in hospital, Nancy said 'I'm so sorry, I didn't mean to upset you, Amber' looking horrified at what her question had caused.

'No, no, I'm fine' Amber said brushing away her tears. 'Sometimes, thinking about my mother just comes over me like that.'

She hurried on 'I also have a job here with a care company who supply carers to go into homes for those who need care but do not need to be in hospital. I don't actually do the care work but I write company policies and do other administration. However, being involved in the company makes me feel as though I am doing something to help others.'

Nancy nodded at her comments and Amber asked her 'How did you and Jonathan meet, if I may ask?'

'We met at Uni when we were both taking business management degrees'. Nancy continued 'We took some enormous financial risks but it seems to have worked out well for us.' She smiled broadly at Jonathan.

Jonathan responded 'I couldn't have done it without you' and then raised his glass to her saying 'Chin, chin'. They all clinked their glasses together in a mood of camaraderie.

They moved indoors as dusk began to fall and the temperature started to drop. Alex looked at Amber and was pleased that she liked his neighbours so much but felt absurd as he realised he was feeling anxious again that he might lose Amber, but couldn't work out why.

He was feeling perturbed because he had actually discreetly followed her the other night after she had left his apartment back to her home about a 10 minute walk from the seafront. He was annoyed with himself but felt compelled to do this, but without understanding why.

❀

A while later, as the first stars began to shine in the evening sky, Harriet swept into the flat, changing the atmosphere in the room quite dramatically. Nancy introduced her to Amber who got a slight smile from Harriet who otherwise appeared uninterested in her sister's guests.

Alex moved over to stand closer to Amber feeling he needed to protect her and Amber felt a distinct reserve toward Harriet, bordering on dislike, which she found astonishing. She had never met her before but felt an aura around Harriet that she found uncomfortable. Alex had briefly updated her about Harriet's notoriety, but Amber felt there was something else that deeply disturbed her about Harriet.

Jonathan appeared not to notice anything, pouring Harriet a glass of champagne. Harriet thanked him perfunctorily and immediately launched into a monologue of her day. Apparently she was annoyed at the beggars sitting on the ground begging in Western Road snorting 'Peasants, making the place untidy, I am surprised that they are allowed to do that, why can't something be done about it?'

She ploughed on about the rest of her day's

activities without waiting for an answer to her question.

Amber privately disagreed with Harriet about the beggars thinking sadly of these people unable to keep a home or look after themselves, especially if they had mental health issues. She thought especially about one of the homeless men who offered to read out his poems to people in return for a few coins.

Nancy leaned back on the leather sofa with a resigned look on her face as her younger sister carried on talking to them without any interest in their welfare whatsoever.

Then, as Jonathan joined his wife on the sofa, lounging on it with one of his long legs over the arm, Amber saw the strangest thing.

She blinked hard but could still see Jonathan as a louche young man dressed in the same clothing worn by the people in Versailles, which she had researched after hearing about Alex's regression.

She shook her head impatiently as the vision cleared and heard Jonathan asking if she was all right as she had gone rather pale. She smiled back at him, saying she was fine and thanking him for his concern.

As she thought about the photograph of Nancy's grandparents which she had seen on the cabinet earlier, she felt a little troubled.

They had looked so familiar but she dismissed her thoughts as fanciful at the time, as she had never met them.

Now, however, with the vision of Jonathan and the photograph, Amber was beginning to worry about herself. She drank more champagne thinking that later, when she was alone, she would consider more of what she had seen and felt here.

Harriet was still talking, saying that she had heard footsteps echoing behind her in the car park when she had taken a shortcut and thought it may be the paparazzi following her again after articles had appeared in the newspapers about her and her famous married lover.

'Why did you have to get involved with him?' Nancy said angrily, an annoyed look on her face. 'You could stop seducing men who are committed to others and you knew this one had a wife and four small children as he is a well known member of Parliament'.

When Nancy got no immediate response, as Harriet remained stone faced, she sighed 'Hat, I guess you are free to make any decision you wish, but there are always consequences from what you do.'

Harriet looked at her older sister and brazenly said 'I don't see why that is my problem, he could always have said no' as she finished her glass of champagne and set it down on the table.

'I have things to do, so don't bother including me for dinner. I am going for a dip in the hotel swimming pool first' she said, as she left the room with a haughty swagger, smoothing her tight dress down as she went.

Nancy gritted her teeth but Jonathan laid a hand on her arm. Nancy looked pained at her younger sister's behaviour and wished heartily that she could do something to change it. 'I worry about her so much, and I try and talk to her but she doesn't take any notice of me.'

No one yet knew how these events would play out.

Jonathan though was not quite as concerned with his sister in law's behaviour as he felt that any publicity for his club was no bad thing, despite having a club privacy policy for his club members. Not a thought he would share with Nancy though.

Nancy gave him a kiss on the cheek saying 'Oh pour me another glass of champers before I throttle her then, darling'.

Meanwhile, Alex and Amber were sitting together on the sofa their hands entwined.

Nancy looked at them fondly before remarking quietly to Jonathan that at least some people were sincere in relationships. Jonathan smiled at her, raising an eyebrow at her comment, thinking that Nancy was ever the romantic one.

When should I pay?

You must pay if none of the statements apply to you on the day you were asked to pay. These are the only accepted reasons for not paying.

I'm not sure if I should pay

Pay and ask for a **prescription refund form (FP57).** You can't get one later. If you find you didn't need to pay, you can claim a refund up to 3 months later.

What if I don't pay when I should?

We check claims made for free prescriptions. If we can't confirm that you are entitled to exemption from prescription charges, you may be issued a Penalty Charge Notice and you may have to pay up to £100 as well as your prescription charge(s), and you could be prosecuted.

Can I get help to pay?

Help with costs may be available. You could also save money by buying a prescription prepayment certificate.

Check at **www.nhsbsa.nhs.uk/check**

Is my exemption certificate still valid?

Visit www.nhsbsa.nhs.uk/exemption to see what help is available or ask at your GP surgery or pharmacy.

I am unable to collect my prescription

If you are unable to collect your prescription someone can do so on your behalf. Your representative should complete the 'If you paid' box and sign the form, or you or your representative should complete the 'If you didn't pay' box, and your representative should sign the form. Your representative will need to put a cross in the 'on behalf of patient' box next to their signature.

Why did the pharmacy ask to see evidence?

We need to check your exemption is valid.

The NHS Business Services Authority is responsible for this service. We will use your information to check your exemption is valid, pay the dispenser and help plan and improve NHS services. Find out more at www.nhsbsa.nhs.uk/yourinformation

Mrs Gertrude Catherine
Fletcher
NHS Number: 4660504255
DoB: 22/01/1928
Flat 8 Maple Court St Georges
Park Ditchling Road
Burgess Hill
West Sussex
RH15 0SW

Practice Pharmacist

BROW MEDICAL CENTRE
The Brow Medical Centre The
Brow
Burgess Hill
West Sussex
RH15 9BS

Chapter 12

I t was a lovely sunny morning and the sun was sparkling on the sea, although the wind was cold.

Nancy and Amber were sharing coffee at Nancy's apartment after having been to a yoga session together at the Brighton Buddhist Centre in the North Laines, A mutual passion they had discovered.

As Nancy put the coffee cups on the coffee table, she looked at Amber and smiled. 'I don't know why but I feel like I have known you before. I don't think we have met before, have we?'

Amber responded 'That is so interesting, as I feel the same way, but I am sure we haven't met before now.'

Amber put her fingers to her lips wondering whether to share with Nancy the image which had come to mind the other night of Jonathan dressed in French clothing.

'What is it?' Nancy asked, a small frown on her face.

Amber looked at Nancy and answered her question with another.

'Do you remember that night we were drinking champagne here and Jonathan asked me if I was alright as apparently I had gone pale?'

'Why yes, Harriet was being a real pain and a worry to me as I remember. What was it about that particular evening?'

Amber explained that she had seen Jonathan dressed in different clothing and thought it was from a period in Versailles in the 1700s.

She explained further 'After Alex's regression when he said he had been in Versailles, I looked it up on the internet to find out more information and Jonathan was dressed in similar clothing to one of the pictures I saw.'

Nancy was clearly intrigued with the idea. 'Alex has talked about the regression therapy and I find it very interesting.'

Well do you like all things French, as I do? Nancy continued, ' I have always enjoyed French food and their architecture, especially Versailles and the Louvre, although I hate the glass pyramid in such close juxtaposition to the old buildings there. '

Before Amber could respond, they heard the sound of a key turning in the front door lock.

Jonathan open the door, his keys jingling as he put down his large bag. 'Hi ladies, what are you gossiping about then?' he queried.

Nancy looked a little piqued. 'We were talking about whether we had lived in France in another lifetime together, if you must know.'

Jonathan replied 'Really?' He looked at Nancy's annoyed expression quickly continuing 'Interesting thought maybe. Well, you have always loved the French way of life, haven't you, darling?'

Nancy nodded, before asking 'Been buying your own birthday present then,?' as Jonathan came over and gave her a quick peck on the cheek.

'Of course, but that doesn't preclude you buying me more' he grinned, as he turned back to his package, a painting he had just purchased from an art shop in the The Laines.

'What have you bought?' asked Amber as he tore off the brown paper off of his purchase.

'It is a limited edition of William Russell Flint's picture of two women by a water mill in France called The Mill Pool, St Jean de Cole' he replied, smiling broadly at her.

Amber thought it was charming and Nancy commented that it was just like him to want pictures of half naked women on the wall.

'Where do you think we can put it up?' Nancy enquired, looking at the large windows which left little wall space for hanging pictures.

'I think it would look good in our London house.' Jonathan replied.

'Just as well we have the 4 x 4 here and not the Porsche as we wouldn't get all our stuff back to London' commented Nancy as Jonathan held up the picture continuing to admire his new acquisition.

She turned and smiled at Amber, 'Oh I know, you and Alex must come up to London to Jonathan's fiftieth birthday party, it's planned for two weeks time. We have to go back to London as we have had quite a long break here. We are having a fancy dress party and it would wonderful if you came too. Please say you will come' she looked at Amber expectantly.

Amber grinned delightedly 'Yes, I don't have any commitments that far ahead, so I would love to and I will check if Alex is free. That would be so much fun.'

'That is brilliant. We will have a dinner for about twenty of us first and then others will join the party later' Nancy said, her face showing her pleasure.

Nancy then put her hand on Amber's saying 'We are so pleased that Alex has met you, you make a great couple.'

Amber blushed slightly but was pleased that Nancy felt the same way as she did about her relationship with Alex.

The sun went behind a cloud and at that moment, as Amber looked at Nancy she thought she saw shadows behind her.

Chapter 13

Alex and Amber had discussed at length what to wear to Jonathan's party and finally decided to go with costumes from 18th century Versailles, after Amber's discussion with Nancy about their interests in France.

They were able to find their outfits in a fancy dress shop in the historical town of Lewes, about a fifteen minute drive from Brighton.

On the day of the party they arrived at the costume shop having reserved their costumes in advance. Amber was delighted with her costume but disappointed that that there were no wig to go with it.

Unhappy that she wouldn't be able to finish her outfit off properly, she talked with the owner of the small shop who assured her that no wig was required, as women didn't wear wigs at that time.

Amber asked her 'Which period of French history does my costume represent then?'

The shop owner, a petite lady in her late fifties, warmed to her theme. 'This costume would come from the French Court of Louis XV and the hairstyles at the time were of curls close the head, not wigs. Let me show you some pictures' she continued, pulling out a thick book of pictures of costumes from the bookshelf next to the counter.

She leafed through quickly and found a picture of Madame de Pompadour and showed Amber how her hair was styled. She continued 'The Marquise was a trend setter in her day both in dress and artistic pursuits as well as keeping the King amused as he was prone melancholy.'

'Oh look' exclaimed Amber 'she is wearing the same colour dress very similar to mine.'

The shop owner was enjoying sharing the historical information with Amber who was fascinated by her knowledge.

Amber went to one of the small fitting rooms and tried on her costume. It had a full skirt and tight bodice with a square neckline made in grey silk with a lavish amount of pink ribbons, lace and flowers down the front. She would have preferred the dress to be in her favourite colour, blue, however she thought that she looked quite presentable in the pale grey dress. She came out of the changing room and turned this way and that, looking at herself in the full length mirror. Alex gave a little whistle as he saw her and she beamed in delight at him, now dressed in his costume.

Alex had had no problem with completing his outfit of a dark green coat, with an elaborate waistcoat, jabot, breeches, stockings and buckled shoes together with a wig.

Amber walked over to him and touched his wig. 'I like that, although it makes you look so different and yet at the same time so familiar' she mused.

The shop owner smiled at them. 'You look so right together dressed like that, may I suggest I take a photograph for my book of costumes and you can have a copy of the photo for yourselves?'

Alex and Amber readily agreed and the owner found some hair slides and they quickly styled Amber's hair into curls to complete her transformation.

Alex and Amber duly travelled to London for Jonathan's party checking into a Belgravia hotel close to Jonathan and Nancy's luxurious London home in Eaton Square.

Amber was delighted with their large hotel room with its luxurious bathroom and bedroom and views from the window. He smiled at her, and grabbing her he fell onto the large bed before kissing her.

A few hours later, Amber giggled when the taxi driver did a double take at their fancy dress clothing as they got into the taxi to go to the party.

Alighting from the taxi ten minutes later they walked up to the front door, between two large pillars and used the heavy knocker. The door swung open by a footman wearing a wig, coat and breeches.

Amber gasped in astonishment as the footman was also dressed in clothes of the same time period.

Amber cried out in delight when Jonathan and Nancy greeted them dressed too in the same Versailles fashions as themselves. Although it made her shiver to see Jonathan resplendent in very similar clothes, a dark red coat over a gold waistcoat, to the vision she had had of him in their Brighton apartment.

They laughed together about the coincidence as they took flutes of champagne from the tray held by another footman. 'I decided we would dress like this' Nancy confided in Amber, 'After our talk in Brighton the other week about the possibility of being together in France all those years ago. I thought it fun that the waiters could be dressed as Versailles footman too.'

Amber smiled back 'That is exactly why I thought we would dress like this too' she responded. 'I love your pearl necklace by the way.'

Nancy smiled back, fingering the pearls. 'Yes, I have always loved pearls, you know'.

Amber then looked into the room in front of

them where some other party guests were drinking champagne. The room was large with colours of blue and gold. There were dark blue curtains at the full length windows, delicately patterned pale blue and gold wallpaper, paintings, antiques and beautifully upholstered furniture.

She saw the picture that Jonathan had bought as his own birthday present right in front of her in the hallway, a small light above illuminating it.

She looked at Jonathan. 'Your picture looks great there, doesn't it?'

Jonathan looked pleased that she had noticed, nodding in agreement.

Then they looked up as Harriet appeared at the top of the staircase, clearing her throat so they would notice her. She walked elegantly down the stairs in a diaphanous white off the shoulder dress, her dark hair pinned up and wearing a quiver of arrows on her back, holding a bow in one hand.

Jonathan looked up grinning 'Oh, Diana, Goddess of the Hunt then'.

Harriet looked at him with a hint of a smile before walking past them into the drawing room. Nancy's eyes widened at the transparency of her sister's dress.

Amber thought she looked beautiful but found her demeanour somewhat cold. She thought unkindly that Jonathan's comment was right on point as she felt that Harriet did hunt down her prey, especially after her recent notoriety with the married MP.

Harriet caused a stir as she entered the room with many of the male guests openly appreciating her flimsy outfit, which was exactly the effect she had planned to create.

The four of them followed Harriet into the drawing room and although several men immediately gathered around Harriet, she moved away and came over to stand by Alex.

Amber wanted to ignore her, however she was fully aware that Harriet seemed to be taking a great interest in Alex, constantly touching his arm as she talked, smiling up at him from beneath her dark lashes.

Amber instinctively drew back alarmed at her feelings of jealousy as she watched Harriet toying with Alex, which she couldn't really understand. She moved closer to Alex slipping her fingers into his, just as a gong sounded to take them into dinner.

The dining room had red brocade wallpaper giving it an intimate feel, with the long dining table beautifully set with bowls of flowers and candelabras, whose candles lit up the sparkling tableware.

The food was delicious and there was a lot of laughter as people made speeches about Jonathan to which he responded in kind.

After the sumptuous meal was finally over, Nancy, Amber and Alex were sitting on one of the pale gold leather sofas at the end of the long drawing room, the chandeliers glowing, glasses chinking and laughter and conversation all around them, as other guests arrived, filling up the room.

Nancy looked up as one of her guests approached, a large man with a ginger beard dressed as Henry V111. 'Oh, Roland, darling, you look amazing, just like the pictures of him'.

'Thank you, my dear, may I return the compliment? You look stunning yourself''.

Nancy was dressed in a peacock blue dress similar to Amber's in design with lots of lace and ribbons adorning it.

'Thank you Roland, you are very kind' she responded.

Roland was a well known psychic to the rich and famous in London circles. He continued 'I had to come and talk to you three, my psychic antennae are quivering, you know'. Nancy smiled at him, well used to his ways.

'Do tell' she encouraged him.

The noise in the room seemed to recede and Amber felt they were all in a bubble, as Roland sat on one of the arms of the sofa, his eyelids starting to flutter as he spoke quietly but with authority.

'My dears, I see a time when you were together in a French court, I think in the 18th century. There was seduction, betrayal,' pausing 'a murder even' he waved his hand in Nancy's direction at that, 'Family connections and friendships. Yes, I see the Palace of Versailles' he paused, 'Louis the Beloved' he frowned, 'I think that is what I am hearing and you Nancy were an important woman there. My dears, there was so much delicious intrigue, jealousy and then it all ended with a murder.'

Roland continued 'The person responsible for a lot of these issues though, isn't here with you at the moment' he looked around distractedly before pausing again. He appeared to be partaking of an inner dialogue, and continued 'but the theme for today is of compassion and forgiveness, I understand.'

He paused again, his eyelids fluttering once more before stopping. Nancy, Amber and Alex were transfixed at what they had heard. Jonathan had strolled over to collect Nancy before making a speech to their guests and had heard most of what Roland had said too.

Roland breathed heavily, 'Well darlings, I think that is all there is for the moment'. As he finished speaking his life partner, a portly man dressed as Samuel Pepys, grabbed his arm 'Roly, come with me, I have found the TV producer we were talking about, you must talk with him' he said urgently.

'Manners, Cecil' Roland replied fondly, smiling at the group as he departed with him.

Jonathan raised his eyebrows at Roland's retreating back saying 'Nancy, time to make our speech, I think' offering his hand to her.

She stood up shaking her head slightly at what she had just heard and taking Jonathan's hand, she moved majestically towards the centre of the room near the full length windows with their heavy drapes, the guests parting to make way for the couple.

Amber looked at Nancy and murmured 'Oh, Aunt Adele.'

She was thinking 'That is not the first time I have seen Nancy taking control of the room like that.'

Alex interrupted her thoughts by handing her a glass of champagne, saying 'Well that has certainly given us something to think about, hasn't it? Wait a minute, did you just call Nancy, Aunt Adele?'

Amber looked at him, unaware that she had spoken.

'Did I, how strange was that? Roland said there were family connections, so if what he said was true, maybe Nancy was my aunt in a previous life in Versailles. You know, we both feel we have known each before now but not understood why. I have always thought that I wanted to call Nancy by a different name too' she concluded.

Chapter 14

That night, in their hotel bedroom, Amber and Alex laughed together hilariously, trying to get each other out of their costumes, before falling on the bed to make love again.

As she fell asleep in Alex's arms, Amber was looking at her French costume hanging on the front of the wardrobe. As her sleep deepened, her mind travelled back through time and she started to dream of Versailles.

Her dream, like her others, was fragmented.

The dream started with her standing inside the Palace of Versailles looking down the Hall of Mirrors with the statues and the mirrors on one side with the windows overlooking the garden on the other. The chandeliers were sparkling in the sunlight below the ornately painted ceiling.

She was wearing a long dress that rustled as she walked and she could hear musicians playing as more people crowded into the Hall.

Then to her surprise, she saw Harriet,dressed beautifully with her dark hair pinned up in curls, flirting with some young men.

There were some fleeting glimpses of events.

She was transported to a dark bedroom where to her horror she saw Alex in bed with Harriet and she felt great distress.

She then saw the same bedroom in the morning and Jonathan was confronting Harriet and Nancy burst in and they were getting angry with each other.

The scene faded before she found herself looking through a window at carriages leaving the Palace, with courtiers going out to be entertained with the King and the Marquise de Pompadour.

It was a view she enjoyed watching. The carnival of carriages and the immaculately groomed horses as they left the Palace gates. She then heard a pistol shot and saw the horses harnessed to one of the carriages were bolting.

She was immediately transported outside and looking down from above, she saw the commotion around the carriage as Nancy's body was found. She saw Jonathan, dressed very differently from his usual Court dress, moving quickly away as he put the pistol inside his coat.

The scene changed again and she was in her private rooms in the Palace. She felt that her mother had died and saw a picture of her on the wall which, when she looked closely, seemed to resemble herself greatly. She then saw someone whom she thought was her father who had come to her to ask her to pray for Nancy's soul. Another scene appeared with the same man and Alex poring over documents together and a third man with presence, who she knew to be the King.

She had a strong feeling that Alex wanted more from her than she was able to give.

Lastly, she saw herself being driven away from the Palace waving goodbye to her father and Alex. She acknowledged some feelings of regret but also of excitement for the future.

The dream faded away but the following morning, as she awoke, Amber recalled her vivid dream. She rolled over in the comfortable bed to see Alex looked down at her smiling.

She grinned back at him taking his hand.

'I must tell you about this weird dream I had last night about Versailles.'

'I'll make us some tea and then you can tell me all about it' he responded.

She lay back against the big white pillow thinking how lucky she was that he was so attentive.

He came back to the bed giving her a cup of tea. He then made himself comfortable next to her and she shared her dream with him.

Suddenly Amber realised why the photograph in Nancy and Jonathan's flat looked so familiar to her. The couple in the photograph looked very much like her father and the picture of her mother in her room from her dream.

Having explained about the photograph she continued 'I have to tell you' she said, 'that I have had jealous feelings about Harriet, being around you but that makes sense now as I had seen you in bed together in my dream.'

He looked at her, shaking his head in amazement.

She continued 'So the last part where I was leaving the Palace now makes sense, as in my regression I was a nun in the same time period. I must have been going to a convent to get away from all the things going on there.'

She carried on 'I believe you were in love with me and wanted to get married but I left instead' she said smiling, giving Alex a soft punch on his arm.

Alex looked at her in amazement. He thought for a moment and then said 'That makes so much sense. I have to tell you, I have had this underlying fear from the minute I first met you, that you would leave me as you did before. I couldn't understand it, not at all.'

He shook his head again as he shared his feelings with her.

Amber bit her bottom lip at that comment and said 'Wow.'

Not quite knowing how to respond to Alex's fears she quickly said 'Shall we share this with Nancy and Jonathan? I know Nancy is very interested in all things French and I am sure she would love to know about this. What do you think?'

'I think we had better get over our hangovers first before we talk to them he said laughing, 'Let's shower and go down and get some breakfast'.

They were unaware of the events unfolding at their party hosts home.

Fortified by full English breakfasts, Amber and Alex returned to their hotel room to finish packing before checking out. Alex's mobile rang just as they stepped back through the door.

Alex answered the call and held his hand out to Amber who immediately came and stood next to him to listen in on the call.

'Thank goodness you are still there, Alex' Jonathan said 'Nancy is in hospital with what they think is a heart attack, although from what the doctor was saying, it isn't too bad, I think.'

'No worries, give us the address and we will come straight over' responded Alex. Amber nodded in agreement.

'Thanks, mate, could do with a bit of support, this has scared me silly, I have to say.'

We will be there just as soon as we can grab a taxi' Alex replied, already moving his suitcase off of the bed.

They met in the private hospital and found Jonathan at Nancy's beside where she was hooked up to monitors. She smiled weakly at them at their arrival. 'Sorry about all this nonsense'.

Amber leaned over and gave her a kiss, saying 'Please don't worry, we just wanted to make sure you were okay.'

Alex chimed in 'You gave such a good party it has obviously taken a lot out of you, Nancy.' Nancy gave another small smile, shifting her position in her bed.

'We aren't allowed to stay long but just wanted to see you' Amber reassured Nancy.

Amber held Nancy's hand and they spoke quietly while Alex and Jonathan disappeared together onto the roof balcony for a cigarette.

'What an amazing night that was' said Amber 'but I am sorry to see you like this'. 'I am sure I will be fine, it is just that I feel so tired at the moment' was Nancy's reply.

Amber then gave Nancy an abbreviated

version of her dream about how they had all been connected in Versailles and it seemed that Jonathan had taken his revenge on her by shooting her in the heart.

Nancy looked at her astonished. 'I must tell you that Jonathan and I had a talk the other week and listen to this, Jonathan said that he had always felt responsible for me and particularly my health, but he didn't know why.'

Nancy squeezed Amber's hand, 'but I did tell Jonathan that although he hasn't always been faithful to me, he has been a kind husband.'

Amber looked slightly shocked at Nancy's laissez faire attitude to Jonathan's behaviour but Nancy, looking at her face, said 'I have always felt that we belong together, so I never worried about him. I didn't really want to be with him at first, but it was all so compelling. I had to have this relationship with him.'

Amber looked at the heart monitor in alarm as it beeped 'Oh, okay Nancy relax, I don't like the way your heart beat is rising' .

Nancy lay back on her pillows 'Oh don't worry, love, I am sure I will be fine, I just need to sleep now'.

As Nancy closed her eyes, a serene feeling came over her. Harriet came to mind and she had a strong intuitive sense that Harriet would eventually learn to get her life back on track.

She felt she could let go of the responsibility of looking out for her now.

A dark haired nurse came briskly into the room 'Time's up, I'm afraid, my patient needs her rest.' she said in her soft Irish accent.

She checked Nancy's pulse, looking at the monitor before looking at Amber to make sure she had the message to leave.

At that moment, Jonathan and Alex returned to the room, so Amber and Alex quickly took their leave, assuring Jonathan that they were there for them and only a telephone call away. Jonathan smiled his thanks and looked back at Nancy who had already dozed off.

Jonathan returned home later that day to encounter Harriet wandering around the living room holding a half full bottle of champagne in her hand.

In response to Jonathan's look Harriet, slurring slightly, said 'I went to the hospital but they said that Nancy was sleeping and couldn't go and see her yet. They actually stopped me from going in' her voice rising in indignation as she raised the bottle to her lips and took a large gulp of champagne.

Jonathan sat down heavily on one of the chairs and just waved her away. He was fed up with her behaviour and how anxious it had made Nancy. He was sure that Harriet would have caused an enormous fuss at the hospital but he was too tired to think about Harriet and her concerns.

Harriet stumbled over to him saying 'I will hold you responsible if she doesn't get well, she can't leave me again' before bursting into tears. Jonathan didn't comprehend why Harriet would think that, but put it down to her being drunk.

Wearily, Jonathan stood up and put his arm around Harriet's thin shoulders, taking the champagne bottle away from her. 'Go and have a sleep and I am sure you will see her in the morning'.

Harriet, for once, obeyed his suggestion, meekly going out of the room, sniffing as she did so.

Chapter 15

The hospital corridors and wards dim with low lighting, were quiet as the night moved on, when suddenly alarm bells started ringing from Nancy's room, breaking the silence.

It was just after 2am when the telephone rang next to Jonathan's bed. Fumbling with the light and picking up the phone, Jonathan had a dire feeling of dread which was confirmed when a doctor informed him with regret that Nancy had suddenly taken a turn for the worst and they hadn't been able to save her, despite their prompt efforts at her bedside.

Jonathan run his fingers through his hair hoping against hope that this was part of a dream groaning 'No, no, this can't be'.

Jonathan crushed his hand around the phone as the call ended. He sat up shaking, sweat trickling down his face. This was his worst nightmare.

Later that day, Alex and Amber were back at Jonathan's Eaton Square home, sitting with him on one of the sofas. Jonathan leaned back squeezing his eyes shut and Amber felt a tremor of emotion run through his body. All she could think to do was to hold his hand.

He was dressed in jeans and black suede loafers but was still in the burgundy silk dressing gown with the initial J monogrammed on the front pocket in gold thread that Nancy had bought him for his birthday. Amber looked at the bottle of whisky and his half full glass in front of them on the coffee table. She didn't know what to say.

Alex looked over at Jonathan and said 'We are so sorry, Jono. We are always here for you. Call us at any time, promise?' Jonathan looked at Alex nodding slightly saying 'I just can't take it in'.

Amber looked at him and thought he was about to cry.

At that moment, Harriet appeared in the doorway, looking like a contrite schoolgirl in a short frock, her cheeks smeared with mascara from where she had been crying.

She came over to the other sofa saying, her voice rising 'What am I going to do now that Nancy has gone? I caused her so much distress but I didn't think about her and now she is dead because of me.' She burst into tears again repeating 'What am I going to do now?'

Jonathan lay back with his eyes closed and said nothing.

Alex took it upon himself to say 'I am sure Nancy loved you Harriet and has more than forgiven you. You must try and forgive yourself too.'

He hesitated, not knowing if he should say more, but then continued 'What is important is our reaction to things and how we handle the consequences.'

Harriet didn't quite follow his reasoning but said 'Oh my God, that is one of the things that Nancy used to say to me about what I did and the consequences and I just didn't listen.' She burst into tears again.

At that moment the half open door was pushed open further as Nancy's newly acquired dachshund puppy, called Poppet, struggled in with one of Nancy's sweaters in her mouth.

Jonathan opened his eyes at the noise of Poppet's claws on the wooden floor and looked at the new arrival.

'Oh no, I knew she was unhappy without Nancy around but now she is ruining her best sweater' he said, starting to get up to take the clothing away from the puppy.

Amber put her hand lightly on Jonathan's arm, 'Maybe let her be. A friend of mine had a dog who would only settle in her basket if she had her owner's shirt with her while he was away.'

Jonathan sat down again shrugging his shoulders 'Whatever you think' he said dispiritedly. Amber looked back at him, seeing how haggard and grey he looked.

Harriet bent down and picked up the puppy and sweater, putting the little dog on her lap where she settled down immediately wagging her tiny tail before closing her eyes.

Harriet however couldn't resist talking further. 'But what am I going to do without Nancy? She was my anchor.'

Amber then got up and and went over to the other sofa to sit beside Harriet. 'We all make mistakes, but that is why we are here, to learn and grow, so try not to judge yourself.'

She paused 'You can always come and talk to us if that will help.'

Harriet looked at her as more tears rolled down her face.

Harriet said 'I do what I do, because I want people to notice and admire me, but all I caused was more hurt.' More tears slid down her cheek.

Alex looked at her kindly and said 'Awareness is the key: awareness of yourself and of others and how you treat them. You are giving away your power by looking to others for validation'.

Harriet looked at him uncomprehendingly.

Amber looked at Alex and Harriet and then shot him a look as if to say 'too much information, too soon'.

Alex nodded back, understanding, as he too saw the look on Harriet's face.

Jonathan looked at his sister in law, taking a deep breath then letting it out in a deep sigh.

'Hat, we all probably seek approval whether we are aware of it or not'.

He looked at Poppet asleep on her lap. 'Just look after the puppy, it will give you something else to think about. What you give out, you get back.'

Harriet looked at him before giving him a wobbly smile as she continued to stroke the puppy's sleeping head.

This seemed to use up what little energy Jonathan had and he sat back on the sofa, closing his eyes again.

Suddenly, he thought he could smell Nancy's favourite Chanel perfume and felt a slight pressure on his shoulder as if she had put her hand there.

He opened his eyes quickly to see if anyone else had noticed but they seemed more focused on Harriet at present.

177

The sun came out at that moment shining throughout the living room.

The angels looked down and smiled at the love and compassion in the room.

Chapter 16

14 months later

Harriet was in the guest bedroom that Nancy had allocated to her long ago at their London house where she had been staying ever since Nancy passed on. Although neither would admit it, she and Jonathan both enjoyed the presence of another person in this big house.

Poppet, having been Nancy's new pet, was now devoted to Harriet and was presently fast asleep on the luxurious white duvet on Harriet's bed.

Harriet's phone vibrated on the bedside table and she saw it was Amber calling.

A few moments after listening to Amber, Harriet gave a little cry causing Poppet to wake up and stare in surprise at her.

When the phone conversation finished, Harriet rushed out of her room and down the curving staircase calling out Jonathan's name excitedly. Poppet jumped down from the bed, following Harriet, barking at the commotion.

Jonathan appeared in the kitchen doorway holding his mobile phone in his left hand and a broad smile on his face.'I have just been speaking with Alex if that is what you want to tell me' he said.

Harriet drew breath and sat down on the stairs looking at Jonathan through the bannister railings.

'A wedding at the Brighton Pavilion and a baby' she exclaimed.

'Whoa, back the truck up. I know about the wedding but nothing about a baby' he exclaimed.

'Yes, yes' said Harriet impatiently. 'Amber has just found out she is pregnant. Oh I am not supposed to have said anything because she is not sure how Alex feels about a baby and hasn't told him yet. Although his mother, Amber says, will be pleased too as she is anxious to become a grandmother.'

Jonathan shook his head 'I know nothing about this.'

'Oh, don't worry, Jono, Amber obviously tells me more than Alex tells you. Alex recently took her up to Weybridge to meet his parents, Carole and Tim, and his younger brother and sister, Philip and Andrea. They all got on famously and Amber is so pleased as she now feels she has a proper family after being an only child of a single mother. That is when Alex's Mum kept dropping heavy hints about grandchildren, although Amber didn't know she was pregnant then.'

Jonathan just shook his head 'Well, I am sure they will get it sorted knowing those two.'

At that moment, Poppet started barking again standing facing the front door.

'Oh, I must take Poppet out for her walk in the park. Would you join me for coffee at the cafe nearby, Jonathan? Their coffee and cakes are to die for' Harriet said standing up.

Jonathan thought of his very expensive coffee machine in the kitchen which made great coffee in his opinion, but made no comment.

Harriet continued 'I would like to run something past you. Would you come?'

'Sure, it that the place in Elizabeth Street?'

'Yes, shall we say eleven o'clock?' Harriet responded looking at her watch.

'No problem, see you there then' he said as he withdrew into the kitchen as Harriet went back upstairs to collect her coat.

The clock on the wall in the cafe showed 11.05 as Jonathan stepped in through the door and looked around.

The place was bright with red checkered tablecloths and a small bouquet of flowers on each table. There was a chalk board by the counter with hand written information about the drinks and specials of the day.

He smiled as he saw Harriet sitting in the corner licking some cream off of her fingers from the profiterole she was already eating.

Poppet jumped up to him, as he sat down at the table. 'Sorry, can't resist these cakes' Harriet said smiling back at him. Jonathan thought she looked so much better, and her face softer, now she had put a little weight on over the past year.

Jonathan, having ordered his coffee and cake from the young waitress said 'What was it you wanted to ask me then? Harriet prevaricated 'What do you think of this place?'

'Looks busy and the food on offer look excellent' he replied.

'I often come here after I walk Poppet and have got to know the owner, Matilda. She has offered me a job here helping out with the accounts and waitressing when they are very busy some lunchtimes.'

'Why not? It sounds perfectly within your capabilities and it would give you something to do'.

Harriet looked at him. 'Good, I wanted to see

what you thought.'

She smiled in satisfaction and changing the subject said 'I have been meaning to ask you, why do you do that part time voluntary work being a porter at the hospital where Nancy was?' Harriet couldn't bring herself to say where Nancy died.

'I am not really sure' Jonathan replied 'but somehow it makes me feel closer to Nancy and I enjoy being anonymous after being at my club where everyone knows me. People at the hospital take me at face value and the older patients love to have a chat.'

He stopped talking as the waitress delivered his coffee and walnut cake.

Harriet looked up 'Oh here is Matilda'. A tall, older woman with dark hair and sallow skin, dressed in a flowing purple kaftan dress came up to their table.

'Oh hello Harriet. Is this Jonathan?' she asked. Harriet nodded.

'I have heard a lot about you' Matilda said as Jonathan looked at up at her, smiling and offering her the chair next to him. Matilda flashed him a smile.

'So, what do you think about helping me out here then?' Matilda asked Harriet.

'I would like that a lot, thank you' was Harriet's response.

'Great, well if you would like to start next week, that would suit me very well' she paused, 'I keep wanting to call you Sophia for some reason, but I do know your name is Harriet.' Matilda shook her head at herself 'I must be losing the plot. Come and see me when you are finished and we can finalise some details.'

She looked up as the bell sounded over the door. 'Oh, more customers, see you in a bit' as she left them to go back to the counter.

The following week, Jonathan was on his schedule at the hospital and was taking an elderly lady back to her room after an MRI scan.

As Jonathan helped her back into bed, she asked him 'Your name is Jonathan isn't it?' He nodded at her as he waited for her to continue.

'Well, listen, my dear' she said looking up at him and taking hold of his hand.

Jonathan looked at his patient with white hair in a fluffy halo around her head, her pale blue eyes and smiled. He was used to the older patients wanting to have a chat and it required very little of him to listen.

184

'You look like a very understanding young man, so I am going to take a chance and tell you this. I am a spiritualist and I see people who have passed on.' She paused, watching for his reaction.

Jonathan gave her a smile. 'My wife was into the paranormal, so I know a little about this stuff' he commented.

This pleased the old lady and she launched into her speech. 'Well, every time I see you, I also see a blonde lady standing next to you and I know that she had close ties with you. I think her name begins with an N.'

Jonathan took a deep breath. 'Oh, so you know who I am talking about then, dear.'

Without pausing, she continued 'Well she wants you to know that she had a very good life with you, however she doesn't want you to be alone now and there is another lady who could make your life happy once again. In fact, I think you may have already met this lady or at least she knows of you.'

Jonathan felt goose pimples rise on his arms as he heard her words but couldn't think of anyone he had met recently that would interest him.

'So, my dear, now that I have given you your message, please pass me my glasses and I will get back to my library book'.

Jonathan was a bit nonplussed at the abrupt change in direction of the conversation but took this as his cue to leave.

Harriet found that she was enjoying her job more than she had anticipated. The hours were from 10am to 4pm which suited her late rising habits and Poppet came in for a lot of attention from the customers.

Harriet began to know the regular customers and enjoyed having a chat with them when she wasn't working on the cafe's accounts.

There was John, an elderly gentleman, who always doffed his hat at her when he came in. He sat at the same table with his pot of tea and proceeded to complete the Times crossword most days.

Daphne, an older lady, came in quite regularly too. She was a petite lady who had a fondness for hats which she ensured matched the colour of her coat, Harriet had observed.

Then there was Sandra, a woman about Harriet's age, who Harriet learned was a carer to an elderly woman in one of the houses nearby. She would come in for a cup of tea, three times week once her shift work had finished. She discovered that Sandra was married to Gary, a class mate from school and they were saving up for a deposit to buy a property. Harriet felt a little sad as she knew that would eventually mean them moving away as house prices in London where beyond their price range.

Harriet had noticed once or twice that Sandra has bruises on her face and neck which she tried to cover with make up. Harriet didn't feel it was her place to pry but the next time Sandra came in, Harriet could see that she held her arm stiffly.

As it wasn't too busy, Harriet sat down at Sandra' table. 'Sandra, what is going on? I am sorry to intrude but I have seen the bruises and now your arm looks to have a problem too'.

There was a flash of anger in Sandra's eyes, but then just as suddenly she started to cry.

'Oh Harriet, I love him so much but I can't do enough to please him and now I feel I have no energy left and I am at the end of my tether. He tells me I am clumsy and that I don't wear the right clothes and when he has had a drink' her voice tailed off as she fumbled for a tissue in her handbag 'but he is always so sorry afterwards' Sandra concluded sniffing into her tissue.

Harriet felt incensed that this caring young woman was being physically abused by her husband.

'Sandra, listen to me. This has got to stop.'

Sandra looked at her, her voice rising 'But what can I do?' she wailed.

Harriet said 'Wait here, I will get my coat and tell Matilda that I have to go out. I am taking you to talk to the Samaritans who helped me so much when my sister died. I am sure that they will be able to help you even if only to talk it over. They can also put you in touch with professional people if that is what you want to do.'

As Harriet left to get her coat, Sandra slumped back in her chair feeling that, at last, she was no longer alone with her problems.

A few weeks Harriet later, the weather had deteriorated and it was raining once again. Harriet was not surprised at how busy the cafe was as people in the park would come in to get out of the rain.

John was already ensconced at his table with his crossword when Daphne walked in, shaking her umbrella as she did so. Harriet was at the counter and looked around for a table to offer to Daphne, however every table seemed to be taken.

Harriet then saw that John had a spare seat at his table and this gave her a sudden thought. She quickly went over to John, knowing his gentlemanly manners and asked if he would mind sharing his table today with Daphne to which he readily agreed, getting up as Harriet beckoned Daphne over.

Harriet took Daphne's order and when she returned, she was very pleased to see them both engrossed in conversation over the crossword.

A while later as Daphne was paying her bill, having refused John's offer to pay, she spoke quietly to Harriet.

'Thank you my dear for seating me with John. We are going for a walk in the park together now the rain has stopped. There were other seats available but that was a great idea' she said giving her a little wink.

Harriet shook her head at Matilda who had heard Daphne's words. They watched John and Daphne walk away together and Harriet said 'I didn't think there were any other tables available which is why I asked John if Daphne could sit with him.'

Matilda smiled back at her. 'Oh yes, there was an empty table over there at the back, you matchmaker.'

'Well, I never saw that' Harriet responded, but felt very pleased that she had been instrumental in bringing two people together.

Amber and Alex were walking towards the Brighton Pavilion on their way to finalise the wedding details with the wedding planner. The day was warm and Amber hoped the weather would hold out for the wedding in a couple of weeks time. She squeezed Alex's hand as they walked through the gardens towards the entrance to the Pavilion.

Alex looked at her worriedly and said 'You seem anxious, are you worried about getting married?' His brow creased with concern.

'Oh Alex, I couldn't be happier about marrying you, but there is something I need to tell you.'

He drew her over to a nearby bench and they sat down. 'Tell me please what is it?' he said urgently.

Amber took a deep breath and said 'I don't know how you will feel about this, but we are expecting a baby.'

Alex tense shoulders dropped 'Oh thank God, I thought you were having second thoughts about marrying me'. He paused. 'Wow but that leaves me a bit speechless' looking at her upturned face.

Amber looked back at him helplessly, tears forming in her eyes 'But what do you really think about a baby?'

'I am delighted' he said hugging her tight and kissing the top of her head. 'And Ma will be over the moon.'

Amber couldn't help but cry a little more, but this time with relief at Alex's reaction to her news.

Later that day, having finished his shift, Jonathan stopped by the hospital restaurant for a cup of tea.

He smiled at two of the nurses whom he had seen a few times before. He went over to an empty table and sat down, picking up the newspaper left there.

Brenda, a plump nurse with a cherubic face and red hair nudged her friend in the arm. 'Look there he is, Em, you know you fancy him, go and talk to him now.'

Emily, small and dark haired with green sparkling eyes, said 'No, I can't do that'!

'If you don't, I will' responded her forceful friend.

Emily, took a deep breath and said 'Okay, but if this goes wrong, it is down to you.'

Sandra looked back at her, 'Don't be daft, how could he not be attracted to you?'

Before she could change her mind, Emily stood up and went over to Jonathan's table saying

191

'May I join you?' Jonathan noticed she had a soft Welsh accent.

'Yes, of course' he replied putting the newspaper down.

'You are new here aren't you?' Emily queried.

'Yes, that's right, I do a few days a week here.'

The conversation flowed and after a while, Jonathan had the strangest feeling that he could smell Nancy's perfume again and felt a kiss on his cheek as if she was saying to him 'This is alright with me.'

The day dawned bright and clear for the wedding. Harriet, as bridesmaid to Amber, was helping her make final adjustments to her hair and dress in Amber's flat in York Avenue.

'Oh you look beautiful,' Harriet exclaimed looking at Amber in her long cream lace dress with red and cream fabric roses in her hair.

Amber turned to Harriet and said 'Thank you, but the baby is growing and the dress feels a bit tight around the middle.'

Harriet looked at her and said in a mock serious tone 'Well if you hold your bouquet over your bump, no one will ever know.'

This struck Amber as hilarious as everyone knew she was pregnant and she laughed until tears came to her eyes.

'Oh, do stop, you are making me cry with laughter and it will ruin my make up'.

She hugged Harriet who was laughing too 'I am so pleased that we have become such good friends.' Harriet responded 'I am thrilled too. You and Alex have been so kind to me. You have shared so much with me, especially your spiritual ideas so now I have a completely different view of life. I am just so grateful to you both.'

Amber gave her a warm smile as the intercom buzzed, alerting them that the wedding car was waiting downstairs to take them to the ceremony and Harriet darted off to answer it.

The wedding was taking place in the Red Drawing Room at the Pavilion. The room, whose walls were covered in red patterned wallpaper with its ornate columns and ceiling and plush red seating, had enough space for forty guests. One of Amber's favourite classical pieces of music 'The Flower Duet' was playing.

Amber entered the Red Drawing Room, holding her teardrop bouquet of red and cream roses followed by Harriet, wearing a soft yellow dress which suited her dark colouring so well. She walked past the seated friends and family to the table where the celebrant, Alex and Jonathan, as best man, were waiting.

Amber looked at Alex, beautifully dressed in his morning suit with a cream rose in his lapel, and they smiled delightedly at each other.

She looked around at all the people gathered there. Alex's family, his mother already holding a handkerchief to her eyes. There was Matilda dressed in a purple suit and a large hat with soft feathers.

She saw Emily, looking at Jonathan adoringly and was very pleased that she had suggested that he bring her to the wedding too.

Amber looked at Harriet who was smiling back at her, both knowing that they were starting on the next stage of their lives, as the marriage celebrant started to speak.

THE END

Author's Note:

I have tried to keep the historical facts of Versailles correct but my characters in Versailles, Brighton and London are all fictional.

Also by Mary Bishop

Alchemy of the Soul – learning to dance
with your own Divinity!

What Am I Doing Here?
A journey through Gaia

Available to purchase through
www.marybishop.co.uk

Alchemy of the Soul -

learning to dance with your own Divinity!

By Mary Bishop

This is Mary's first book, published in 2016 which is an autobiographical account of her life. The narrative shows how awareness of our actions, deeds and words can affect us and the effect we can have on others.

Mary states that we are the only ones who can define our lives and master ourselves thereby determining what our lives can become using the wisdom we hold within. This is Alchemy.

The aim of this book is to show you the way to explore the spiritual realm.

Mary explains how operating from a spiritual level rather than an ego fear based one is a much more powerful way to live. This book can help you reconnect with your soul making you feel empowered and loved bringing more happiness into your life.

Mary invites you to share the journey of her life and its lessons she has learned along the way.

Reviews:

An easy to read, well written book with a lot of layers. Mary shares her personal life journey and there is much to be gleaned from her spiritual teachings. Thank you, Mary, for your honesty, guidance and wisdom. Split into different parts, part 3 gives guided meditations which are a big help and can be sourced on YouTube.

It is so generous of Mary to share her personal story in this book, which I gained so much from reading. I have come to Mary when I have been lost and she has always offered me comfort and shown me possible ways forward with her spiritual light. Through her book I understand her own journey and the depth of her wise counsel.

A wonderful book for anyone who wishes to understand themselves better. It is a revelation of another world. A world just as real as the material world, in which we live. Mary is a very spiritual person, who has helped many people over many years.

It is brave of her to share some very private experiences. Well done. I believe many people will benefit from reading this book. It certainly opened my eyes to a few things.

There is guidance for all in this insightful book, which is full of wisdom for life's journey. It is a

clear and succinct manual for spiritual growth -
a fascinating, unique and soulful book.

Wise words from a very wise woman, easy
reading enlightening material, I highly
recommend to anyone looking to understand
soul purpose.

The ancient science of Alchemy was never really
about turning physical lead into physical gold.
It was really about turning the psychological
dross and negativity (psychological lead) into
spiritual gold. The alchemical symbols used
physical analogies to convey the message. And,
this book takes this approach.

If one alchemizes the psyche, one will have
all the gold that one needs. It would be just a
natural side effect.

This book is part memoir, part spiritual teaching,
part lessons in Tarot and spirituality. She takes
the stages of the alchemical process and applies
it to her own life - and this makes it vivid and
real. We are given the real life applications of
these concepts.

The book is well written and easy to understand. But don't be deceived by the ease. There are deep spiritual truths here that need meditation and digesting.

Perhaps the most important - and practical - part of the book, is Part 3 where she gives guided meditations for healing, manifesting desires, meeting one's guide, getting daily guidance, forgiveness and other subjects.

People think they are suffering from either a health problem, relationship problems or a financial issue. But these are just masking the real problem - the disconnection from the Divine - the disconnection from Spirit. This is causing all the other issues. This book aims to solve the problem at the root - to reconnect a person to the spiritual realities. Highly recommendable.

WHAT
AM
I
DOING
HERE?

A Journey through Gaia

Mary Bishop

Many of us ask the question: What am I doing
here?

Mary has answered this question, in her own
way, within the storyline of her second book,
her first novel published in 2018.

The book can be read on two levels: one as a simple story and the other, as an allegorical journey of self awareness and spiritual understanding using the Major Tarot cards as a guide.

This story is a walk through the 22 Major Tarot cards (also known as the Major Arcana) where the main character, Isra, can understand the lessons presented to her with the help of the Tarot cards, in order for her to learn and grow spiritually through her lifetime.

"The feeling was becoming irresistible, building all the time. She looked around helplessly as she felt she was standing on the edge of an abyss. The soft lighting around her was warm and comforting yet she had the urge within, which was continuing to become stronger and stronger by the minute, to take this leap into the unknown.

Thoughts whirled around in her head of the consequences of taking this bold action.

She took a deep breath trying to calm herself and analyse the feelings that were making her feel so agitated.

The lights enveloping her were changing now from a soft gentle white moving into sparkling deeper colours of indigo, violet and blue in turn. The atmosphere was feeling more compressed and she was finding her breathing was becoming shallow and more rapid.

Suddenly, without warning, everything was moving beneath her and she felt herself in a whirling vortex, a kaleidoscope of shapes and the colours changing now, from blue to green, then yellow, orange and red, the colours getting darker and darker, the deeper she went down. The vortex was a swirling mass now twisting and turning all the time. Various symbols passed by quickly. She saw the glyph of the female sign and the astrological sign of Leo as everything whirled around her faster and faster until it all became a blur. Then suddenly it became very quiet and the energetic flow stopped.

She became aware that something tumultuous had happened but now she had the overwhelming urge to sleep. As her eyes closed to deep slumber she felt a hand slip away from hers and then she slept for a long time.

She awoke to the sunlight pouring through the windows showing dust motes dancing in the air. She looked around hurriedly wondering where she was. The room was large with heavy furniture: a wardrobe, chest of drawers, writing desk and dressing table with blue curtains at the windows and she realised that she was lying in was a four poster bed. She looked around the room seeing beautiful pictures of Turner-like water scenes hanging from the walls.

She desperately tried to remember what had happened, but nothing came.

'What am I doing here?' she cried out in desperation as she fought down a feeling of panic.

Then there was a knock at the door and she felt her heart leap as though there may be help at hand to explain what was going on with her and why she was here."

❀

Reviews

This is my favourite kind of reading. It's a story - interesting in its own right - but its also educational. We learn in an entertaining kind of way.

This is an esoteric novella. But it reads almost like a lucid dream. The reader is never sure whether these events actually happened or whether Isra, the heroine of the story is merely having a dream. She drops into earth incarnation in a blaze of light - from the upper regions. Apparently she comes in as an adult - a young adult. She has parents and is in luxurious wealthy circumstances. I couldn't help thinking of the story or Adam and Eve who were created by the divine fully adult.

They didn't go through the process of birth, childhood, puberty, adolescence, adulthood. No, boom! They were created fully formed, fully mature. This is Isra. Her story begins here. We go through all the various stages of life and life experience with Isra and we participate in the various life lessons that she learns along the way.

I'm not going to give away the story. You have to buy the book. But every character represents one of the Major Arcana cards. There is the fool (Isra) the Magician, the High priestess, Empress and Emperor. The cards come alive in her story. They are not just 'abstract pictures" but represent powers and faculties of the divine. They are real.

Through interacting with the various characters and through her study of tarot, Isra becomes aware of the meaning of the various events that happen and the meaning of her life.

Isra of course is all of us. This is not a story of some woman who lived 100 years ago. It is a story about you - here and now.

At the end of the book are guided meditations. There are meditations for finding your destiny, meeting your guides, forgiveness, healing and much more. One can access them on You Tube, or right from the book. This is a nice bonus. I think any person searching for meaning in life should read this. But a student of tarot should definitely read this. JP

For anyone who has not been sure about the Tarot, what it is and it's implications this book by Mary Bishop will open up their understandings and help them see life in much more than black and white, and their place within that life. The meditations at the end of the book will open up the meditative process in an easy caring way for all who are seeking. A gift from Mary's heart to yours.

As soon as I finished the book, I went back to the beginning and read it again - there was wisdom I had missed the first time round. Mary is keen to share her knowledge and throws light on life's lessons that we need to understand. It helped me a great deal ... and I look forward to reading it again.

I very much enjoyed reading this book which guided Isra on her spiritual journey with the assistance and guidance of the Major Arcana Tarot cards, which really gave them meaning. It would be a wonderful book for those starting on their spiritual journey. I felt sad when it ended.

A very good read. If like me you're a spiritual person but don't really understand why or how you came to be, this book gives you a some understanding of the journey you're on.

The meditation lessons at the end of the story are extremely interesting and helpful.

Mary's next book

Footsteps in the Sands of Time

My diary of past life regressions

Mary Bishop

This book illustrates how past life regression therapy can give great insights into your current life and how information can be forthcoming from the spiritual realm to help you with your life today.

From a young Italian peasant boy in the Middle Ages to an urchin living in London during Shakespeare's time, a warrior monk during the crusades to a Mayan temple worker, Mary shows through her diary of 13 past life regressions what she learned spiritually from each of her previous lives and how this has helped develop her soul growth.

These 13 detailed past life regressions have been written from the original recordings completed over the course of three years, by Mary and her regression hypnotherapist. They are each fascinating in their own right and factually correct to the time periods visited.

For anyone interested in past life regressions, Mary's book literally opens up a whole new world!

An extract from Chapter 10:

Therapist: Where are you and what is happening now?

Mary: I am in a town square watching a young man performing acrobatic turns on the back of a white horse which has a beautiful red and gold saddle cloth. There are two small dogs also performing in this act. I am standing behind a soldier who is wearing a helmet and metal chest covering.1 The square is close to the port.

T: Do you know what country you are in?

M: I think I am Holland and it is the year 1640.

T: Who are you?

M: My name is Beth. I am part of a household in the town.

T: What are you wearing?

M: I am wearing a white bonnet, plaid shawl and a long skirt.2 I am out shopping and stopped to watch the performance in the town square. Today is a happy occasion but another time I was here, there was someone being burned at the stake for religious reasons. I didn't stop and watch that day.

T: What is happening now?

M: I have returned home now and the my employer is calling me to help her pack as we are moving away. There are political and religious tensions that have been building for sometime and it isn't safe to stay here any longer.3 Her husband is called Thomas and they had two small children, a girl and a boy.

T: What happened on the next important day?
M: I am attending a proclamation of marriage celebration in another city and I see the boy of the house where I live and work, now about seventeen, is dancing with a young woman. His clothing was green with a square white collar.4 I can see that he likes his dancing partner greatly. I am dressed in a dark blue dress with the stand up collar.

T: Can you take me to the next important day?
M: The wife of Thomas is dying and has asked me to marry her husband Thomas as I know the household and children well. I am concerned as I have no idea of intimacy between married people, although I know all about the running of the house and looking after the children. I can't refuse her as she has always looked after me very well and been a considerate employer. She had been unwell for a very long time.

T: Please take me to the last day of your life:
M: I am lying in a four poster bed with green covers and curtains and I move towards a tunnel where white light is shining. I see a light shining at the end of the bed and there is a man beckoning me into this white tunnel of light. The people around the bed fade away and I float up this tunnel.

✸

Verifications:

In the pursuit of accuracy, and to see if the information I had been given was factually correct, I undertook research on the internet which. provided the results below:

1 Soldier wearing a helmet and metal chest covering. How a soldier was dressed in the 1600s.

2 White bonnet, plaid shawl and a long skirt. Typical dress for this time period.

3 Political and religious tensions were building. In 1556 Charles passed on his throne to his son Philip II of Spain. Charles, despite his harsh actions, had been seen as a ruler empathetic to the needs of the Netherlands. Philip, on the other hand, was raised in Spain and spoke neither Dutch nor French. During Philip's reign, tensions flared in the Netherlands over heavy taxation, suppression of Protestantism, and centralization efforts. The growing conflict would reach a boiling point and lead ultimately to the war of independence.

There was the 80 years of war for Dutch independence, 1568 to 1648, which was a revolt against the political and religious sovereignty of Philip the Second of Spain. There was a twelve year truce after which hostilities broke out again around 1619, which finished about 1648, when

Holland was recognized as an independent country.

4 His clothing was green with a square white collar. Typical of this time.

5 Dark blue dress with the stand up collar. Typical of this time.

Regression sessions undertaken with Helen Colbeck, Quantum Healing Hypnosis Technique regression therapist. helen_colbeck@hotmail.com

Why I started my regression journey.

When I was first introduced to the topic of reincarnation, I wasn't very keen on the idea, as I thought life could be fraught enough without having to come back and do it all again in another lifetime!

However, over time it seemed to make sense to me that with all the challenges and difficulties we can face in our day to day lives, we are here to learn and grow at soul level with the opportunities to find out more about ourselves, our reactions and how we interact with others. If we can replace hate and anger with love and compassion then we leave the world a better place when it is our time to return to the spiritual realm.

Having had some difficult memories in young childhood which I presume came from another lifetime, I was keen to learn more of my soul's purpose while being here on Earth. When I discovered regression hypnotherapy, where we can go back to our previous lives, I thought it might offer a multitude of clues to address my early memories and help me while living here.

My first experience of a past life started at 6 years old. When I closed my eyes to go to sleep, I could see visions of a huge tidal wave.

As we lived on a farm behind the South Downs, we didn't have a television and I had never seen a tidal wave in a book, I couldn't understand where this vision came from and I was terrified as I could see it towering above me.

Many years later, I learned through a regression hypnotherapy session, that in a past life I was drowned in a tidal wave caused by a cyclone whilst living on a beautiful tropical island.

After the hypnosis session, I was amazed that I had been able to 'hear' the sound the wind accompanying this tidal wave, and 'feel' the ground vibrating through my feet as the the cyclone rushed in. I could 'hear' the other villagers screaming as they ran for cover, whilst I think I was paralysed with fear and stood on the beach as it engulfed me. I still feel a catch in my throat if I see huge waves on the television or cinema screen. It hasn't put me off wanting to live under palm trees on the beach though!

Later on, I asked these questions as my spiritual odyssey continued, 'What am I doing here? Who am I? Where did I come from?' Did I learn from my previous lives here?'

It has been written that we can form pre-birth contracts with others while in the spiritual realm to go through certain situations and experiences on Earth, often to resolve negative situations that had not been resolved in a previous incarnation with them.

We also do this in order to learn to become more compassionate by seeing the other side of a situation or go through a challenge to learn and produce growth for our souls.

As already mentioned, if we can overcome obstacles, difficult situations with forgiveness and love then we have moved into alignment with our spiritual selves bringing love, enjoyment, health, wisdom and spiritual clarity into our world.

Through the process of regression hypnotherapy, we can gain access to our previous lives. This uncovers a great deal of knowledge from another part of our soul which remains in the spiritual realm, which I call our Higher Self. This knowledge can then be used to heal us in many different ways. Sometimes it appears, we reincarnate very quickly but other times it may hundreds of years before we return to Earth to continue our learning.

In 2015, I did my first hypnotherapy regression session with my friend, Helen, who is a qualified Quantum Healing Hypnosis Technique regression therapist.

Following this session, we did a further twelve hypnotherapy regression therapy sessions over a period of three years, all of which were recorded. The resulting information formed the body of my next book, 'Footsteps in the Sands of Time My diary of past life regressions'.

These thirteen detailed past life regressions have been written from the original recordings and factually checked to be correct to the time periods visited.

At the start of each session, I lay on the bed and Helen took me through a guided visualisation and from there she took me back to a past life. Helen asked me questions: Where was I? What was I wearing? What time period was I in? Then continued asking more detailed questions, to build up a picture of that past lifetime.

In my first session, I found I had been a young male Italian peasant who rose through the ranks of society and helped young homeless boys with accommodation and gave them an education.

At the end of the hypnotherapy regression session, Helen asked me to contact my Higher Self for spiritual information and this was the result from this first regression session we did together.

H: Now it is time to ask some questions of your Higher Self. What are you experiencing?

M: I am 'seeing' a collective group of spirits as we are all connected at our spiritual level. I am told that we have access to all of them. As souls we all have out own pathways, which together form a tapestry of interconnecting energies.

H: That makes sense. What this life was for and what have you learned?

The lesson learned was that out of one kindness comes many. Through the kindness of others and by being taken in, I was then able to help many others. This life was an illustration to others.

I learned that balance is important, seasons come and go, and to bring order out of chaos. Bring the laws of nature into the human world to help balance things out.

The purpose of this life: to teach that things can change from the bottom to the top, it is possible to go forward positively. However, I did not allow myself to become emotionally involved, to give away anything from my inner self, but used my energy to help others in return.

I then asked my Higher Self, "What information did this lifetime hold that was in alignment with my current life?"

This was the answer that we received.

"There was a need to look after the larger community as a way of learning. There will come a lifetime to focus on herself. She has helped many others and learnt hard lessons. She has learnt to look after herself. All is extremely well.

If she doesn't see the greater picture, we are aware of it. She is a good teacher – a lot of soul growth and brings light and love through. By example, to be a beacon of light. Life improves. Learn to accept the pain and turn it into laughter and joy – transmutation and alchemy. Turn the darkness into light, it even affects those on the periphery".

This, then, was the start of my regression journey and I wrote this book in the hope that it would help others find answers that may explain some of the challenges and obstacles experienced.

Lightning Source UK Ltd.
Milton Keynes UK
UKHW020711310122
397961UK00005B/41